ESCAPE FROM RUBY'S RANCH

Ruby's Ranch Book 2

RHONDA FRANKHOUSER

SOUL MATE PUBLISHING

New York

ESCAPE FROM RUBY'S RANCH

Copyright©2018

RHONDA FRANKHOUSER

Cover Design by Ramona Lockwood

Published in the United States of America by
Soul Mate Publishing
P.O. Box 24
Macedon, New York, 14502

ISBN: 978-1-68291-761-9

ebook ISBN: 978-1-68291-710-7

www.SoulMatePublishing.com

For my ever-supportive father

who always believed in me.

I miss our morning talks.

Acknowledgments

Thank you to my friends, family, and readers for helping me make a go of this whole writing career thing. You are my inspiration.

Chapter 1

Momma's blood-curdling scream rang out over the ranch.

Eleven-year-old Katherine jerked upright in bed and listened hard against the quiet night. Augie, the old house's kindly spirit, covered her with his invisible presence.

Crickets and dogs rustled outside her open window but the rest of the night was still. The scent of fresh rain over sagebrush filtered in the warm room, causing the ivory sheers to billow gently against the wooden frame.

"Daddy," she whispered. It had to be.

She kicked away the fluffy down comforter Momma bought when they redecorated her room, then slipped on her robe and ran down the hall, searching for the reason Momma screamed.

The rooms in the house were eerily silent and dark. The clock above the antique stove read 11:15 p.m. The television in the front room flickered black and white shadows, while Johnny Carson did card tricks with a turban on his head.

This was odd. Where was everyone? Augie stayed with her until she hit the kitchen door at a dead run, panic rising in her stomach.

The full moon shined bright across the corrals, illuminating the path toward the barn where she spied a single light aglow from the window above the barn door. She ran so fast, her faithful Labradors, Zeus and Zoë, couldn't keep up. The summer evening settled on her bare skin as a hay scented mist. The animals in the corrals shied away from her in fear.

"Whoa. Stop!" Stan stepped out of the barn and held up a hand as she reached the door.

"Katherine, honey, you can't go in there."

"Why can't I?" She peered up into the sad blue eyes of her father's best friend and saw the first of a million tears he would cry. "It's Daddy, isn't it?" She tried to maneuver around Stan, but he grabbed her by the shoulders and forced her to look at him.

"Yes, sweetheart." His voice halted. "It's your father. I just can't let you see what's happened." His words choked in his throat, until finally, he looked away from her disbelieving stare. Momma's sobs bled through the thick wood planks.

Katherine watched him a second longer, waiting for that comforting smile to spread across his anguished face. Then he'd chuckle and tell her he was kidding, like always. But she saw nothing there except grief and sadness, sheer heartbreak. She knew Daddy was dead.

The ribbons of her heart ripped away as she crumbled to the ground, dissolving in tears. Her waist-length, wavy auburn hair fell in front of her face, shielding her from the harsh reality.

Daddy gone? How could that be? Her best friend, her only confidant in the world, taken from her?

"NO!" she screamed, spooking the horses.

Cricket, Katherine's gentle chestnut quarter horse, trotted over, alerted by her young mistress' distress. Zeus and Zoë, riled now, ran the perimeter of the corral, searching the darkness for whatever might have caused her such pain.

Stan patted Cricket's neck, calming her. "She'll be all right, girl. Go on now." He leaned down and held out a hand for Katherine to take, but she kept her eyes trained on the star-filled sky.

Tears trailed down her cheeks as she imagined surviving ranch life without Daddy. No more flapjacks on Sunday mornings. No more gumballs smuggled to her from his pocket after a trip to town. No more gifts of watercolor paints or pastel chalks for her drawing case. No more glamour magazines for her to dream over.

"Come on, child." Stan urged her again to stand.

Cricket nuzzled in close, nibbling gently against her hand, offering support. The comforting scent of her faithful horse was calming. Katherine cradled Cricket's probing muzzle until the mare was satisfied enough to saunter back to the huddle of horses now watching curiously from the far side of the corral.

"Why, Daddy?" This time quiet, shaking her head in disbelief. "How could you leave me here alone with Momma?" She blinked back the tears and tightened her quivering arms across her chest. A gentle, creative, funny, loving part of her world slipped away and she was instantly consumed by loneliness and sorrow.

Her life would never be the same.

Chapter 2

Katherine huddled in bed, one faithful pup on either side, unable to stop her body from shaking.

Stan sent her inside, away from the scene, to save her a lifetime of haunted memories. As much as she protested, he was right. Some things you can't un-see.

She wanted to remember Daddy as the strong, charismatic cowboy who made everyone smile. When the ambulance carried Daddy's lifeless body away from the ranch, she felt an emptiness she never knew existed. It was so final, so daunting. She'd never see him again.

The moon high in the night sky lit the canvas she'd painted of her and Daddy on horseback. Her technique was amateurish, she knew, hardly recognizable as two riders on horseback, but in her minds' eye, it was a vivid dream. Her first cattle drive with the boys. Her special time with Daddy. The only time she had him all to herself without Momma interrupting their fun with a sensible scowl.

Daddy had taught her everything there was to know about riding. How to be one with your horse and anticipate her actions. When to take a risk and when to lay low. He'd had a magical way with the horses. Katherine could only wish for half his talent and intuition.

Katherine loved him for spending the extra time and sharing his wisdom even if secretly she dreamed of wearing silk dresses and fancy French perfume. Of shopping in expensive boutiques and strolling past famous paintings in uptown museums.

It would've broken Daddy's heart if he knew his little cowgirl didn't love ranch life like he and Momma. She loved the way *he* loved it. It was his passion. Their passion, not hers. She kept it to herself so their relationship wouldn't change. If he knew she wanted to be more of a girly-girl, he would've cut her out of his world so she could explore her dreams. She couldn't have handled that.

But now that he was gone . . . how would she manage living this life? How would she communicate with Momma without his playful mediation through those awkward silences? Daddy would crack a joke when things got too serious. He was the only man on Earth who could lower Momma's defensive facade.

Katherine's heart pounded so fast, she felt it bursting inside her chest. Her eyes had nearly swollen shut from crying. Her head pounded like a hammer against dead wood. Augie hovered, but even he seemed at a loss for how to comfort her through this tragedy.

The quiet of the night mourned with her. No field mice scurried through the tall grasses. No hungry bats fluttered through the air. Even the wind had ceased its soothing song.

The curtains lay flat against the pale green walls with nothing to move them. Zeus and Zoë pressed their warm bodies against her, nuzzling when she'd fidget, trying to untangle the sadness that tied her down.

A shotgun blast shattered the silent night and echoed across the open plains, spooking the cattle and horses asleep in the grazing field. The pups cuddled in tighter when Katherine jerked from her daze. She pulled the comforter to her chin and tried to quiet the renewed quiver of her stomach.

She knew exactly what the shot meant. Momma had discarded the animal that had taken Daddy from them. It was her way and for once, Katherine was glad of it. She'd always hated that stubborn bull. He was determined to win his battles from the start.

Less than five minutes later, the screen door in the kitchen slammed hard against the wooden frame. Momma's booted feet treaded furiously up the long, rose-colored hallway toward her room.

Katherine counted her blessings when Momma didn't come to check on her.

"Oh, thank goodness," Katherine whispered to the pups who licked across her tear-soaked cheeks. She and Momma both needed space and time to understand this night. Neither sympathy nor explanation could give them the answer why this tragedy came to be. This was nothing words could fix.

Mumbled voices echoed through the walls from her parents' bedroom. Katherine couldn't make out what was being said but she felt the sorrow and devastation through the plaster. Who was Momma talking to now that Daddy was gone? Who else would she allow in her sacred space?

Katherine sat up and crept out of her room. The pups fell in quietly at her heels like they were hunting a squirrel.

"How could you let this happen? How am I supposed to live without him? You could have stopped it," Momma yelled, with no response.

Katherine stood quiet in the hallway, waiting for answers that never came. She slid down the wall and laid with her head against her parent's door. Waiting and listening.

She prayed the events of last night were nothing but a horrible dream, and soon Daddy would saunter out of the room, dirty boots and tattered hat, yelling for her like every other morning. "Hurry up, girl, dawn's breakin'. We're wasting time."

But all she heard were Momma's muffled sobs and the crash of glass breaking against the wall.

Chapter 3

Seven Years Later

The glare of eighteen candles sparkled in Katherine's eyes as she made the same wish she'd made every birthday since Daddy died. She wanted off this damn ranch.

She'd counted the days until she could finally leave this place, with or without Momma's blessing. One more night and she could live the life *she* wanted, rather than the one Momma had planned for her. Her suitcase was packed and stuffed in the back of her closet. She'd be gone before first light.

"Kat, you doing anything special for your birthday? Going out?" Casey asked. The best wrangler on the ranch peered across the table with a hopeful stare, as he shoved a piece of cake into his mouth.

Katherine stopped dipping the fragrant vanilla bean ice cream from the metal cylinder and smiled at him, figuring Momma would say no to whatever he might have planned, no matter how innocent. She appreciated the effort and the nerve it took to ask but there was no way. Casey was her hero for trying.

"If not, I'd be happy to take you in-ta town for the Sawgrass Dance going on at the hall tonight." A polite smile crossed his friendly, slightly round face. A mess of sandy blond hair crammed tight into a worn-out cowboy hat too small for his head. His hazel eyes all a-light, seemingly proud of the courage he'd mustered in asking.

"What are you thinking, young man?" Momma asked, pulling the dipping spoon from Katherine's cold hand before it dripped sticky cream on to the floor.

Rube Adams, the owner and matriarch of Ruby's Ranch, scrunched her face into a tight, disapproving scowl. The long, gray hair rolled tight into a bun at the nape of her neck made her look older and meaner than she should. "She's not old enough for dating, you should know that, young man." She placed the spoon into the sink without taking her eyes off Casey.

"Momma, I'm eighteen! I can vote, I can join the army, and I can certainly go to a dance in town." Katherine put a hand on one hip and glared at Momma. This was the final straw. That woman thought she could control Katherine, but those days were gone. And Katherine had the birth certificate to prove it.

Casey shuffled nervously, his gaze darting between the two women before reluctantly settling on Rube. "Oh, no ma'am, it wouldn't be a date. Just going as friends. Thought she might like to give 'em fine new boots you got her a spin." The blush on his cheeks gave away his infatuation, but the honesty of his words disarmed Momma.

Katherine saw a flicker of possibility and changed her tactics. "Oh, a dance, Momma! Please? Casey'll get me back home in time to tuck in the horses."

Katherine stepped closer and squeezed Momma's calloused hands. Hoping. "Please Momma, I'll be okay, I promise."

Momma sighed, her thoughtful brown eyes wide and worried. Katherine watched as the concern moved over her like an ice-cold shower.

Stan shuffled his feet under the table when he saw Momma's anxiety start to bubble.

"Rube, let the kids go dance. It'd be good for 'em to work off some of that energy. What on Earth could it hurt?"

Stan scraped up the last bite of homemade ice cream and licked the spoon. "Besides, we have some business of our own to tend to." He stood to place the blue willow bowl into the sink, then winked when Katherine looked up. Her cheeks reddened.

Momma waved off Stan's flirt then glared back to Katherine and Casey.

Casey withered under her disapproval. "I promise, Ms. Rube, we'll be careful. No funny business. I just thought Kat might enjoy showing off them boots. That's all. Besides, everyone should dance on their eighteenth birthday, don't you think?" Casey winked at her, so quick she might've missed it.

Momma looked them over once more, shook her head again, then let out a breath of surrender.

Katherine knew this was as close to a yes as they'd get from Momma. It took two seconds to gather her birthday gifts, peck Momma on the cheek, and sprint to her room.

She slipped on her new boots and let her hair down from her grandmother's tortoise shell clip. A swipe of strawberry lip gloss, a spritz of lemony Jean Naté, and a pinch of her cheeks, and she was ready to dance the night away.

She crept up the hallway and slipped by the kitchen where Stan and Momma muttered in low voices. Katherine knew if she gave her another chance, Momma'd find a reason to keep her from going.

As Momma washed up the dishes, Stan motioned for Katherine to scoot out the door.

Stan Blocker was her savior. Daddy's best friend from Oklahoma. He'd followed her young parents out to homestead the Kern River Valley some twenty years ago. He was the ranch foreman now but more importantly, he was Katherine's buffer. Stan kept Momma calm and off her back as much as he could manage.

Katherine mouthed a thank you and blew him a kiss, then slipped quietly out the front door and waved for Casey to hurry up.

Casey's eyes lit up when she stepped out on the porch. Her dress clung to her shapely figure, and her long auburn hair waved free in the rose scented breeze. He put the old Chevy into gear and slowly idled up next to the porch so she could climb in. The pups wagged around, swatting their heavy tails against the railing, sensing her excitement.

By the time Katherine hopped into the cab, three of the young ranch hands had piled into the truck bed, and Momma had stepped out onto the porch, hands on hips, the protective scowl back on her face.

"Ten o'clock, young lady. You be back by ten o'clock, or I'll be coming for you myself!" Momma could make the bravest man cower when she used that tone.

"Yes, ma'am," Katherine replied, looking down in frustration. She wanted so much to complain, but she knew better. Her night would be over before it started if she didn't hold her tongue.

"Go," she whispered.

"What's that, Kat?"

"I said, *go*," she whispered louder this time. She reached across the seat and pushed down on Casey's right knee to put pressure on the gas pedal.

For a split-second he froze at the touch of her hand, but quickly realized what she wanted him to do. "Oh, go, got ya!" He pressed down hard and accidentally stirred dust in the air behind them.

"Oh, crap," he said, his eyes wide with concern. "I shouldn't have done that. She's waving her arms and yelling."

"Don't you dare stop," Katherine warned. "Let's go dance."

Once they passed under the RR sign at the end of the driveway, Katherine rolled down the window to let the cool, damp smell of alfalfa filter into the musty cab. She noticed Casey held his breath as she unbuttoned the top button of her pale blue peasant dress. She didn't mean to tease him, but she did hope to give onlookers at the dance the impression she wasn't Momma's little girl anymore.

When they pulled out onto the road, Katherine stuck her head out the window and yelled, "Whoo-hoo, free at last."

The boys in the back of the truck came alive, adding their own hoots and hollers.

She grinned at the only real friends she'd ever known. They'd all grown up together, and they'd witnessed the iron hand she'd lived under. She knew they were excited to celebrate the last night of her youth, before she left the ranch to explore the world beyond.

Chapter 4

Dozens of watermelon candles bathed the town hall in a fragrant, romantic light. A three piece country band, surrounded by bales of fresh-cut hay, played a decent rendition of a Willie Nelson classic. The music was so loud, it vibrated in Katherine's chest.

It was like a dream and she loved every bit of it.

Mason jars filled with sunflowers and sweating glasses of sweet tea and lemonade sat atop tipped barrels scattered around the room. The laughing voices brought a smile to her heart. The positive energy nearly lifted her off her feet. Every person glanced fondly into someone else's eyes, until she stepped through the door. Then all eyes were on her.

Voices quieted and heads turned to stare at her. Even the musicians missed a note.

"Jesus," Casey said, noticing the effect she had on the crowd of ranching families out on the town after a long, hot season.

She took a step back as if she'd been pushed away by a strong, hot wind. "Why are they gawking at me? Do I look funny?" Self-conscious, she reached to re-button the button she'd undone on her dress.

"Oh sweetheart, that's not why they're staring." Casey took her hand. "They just ain't never seen nothin' like you before. Your momma's been hiding you for too long."

Katherine's embarrassment burned hot against the glow of the candlelight. At first, she hid behind Casey, shielded from the room of onlookers, but then she straightened her shoulders and stepped forward. Now was as good a time as any to test her moxie. She'd have no one to hide behind in the real world.

"That can't be it." She frowned at him.

What if he was right? She'd never thought of herself as beautiful, but she'd been noticing some changes. She was filling out her clothes a bit differently these days and people were taking note. Maybe he *was* right.

"So, you gonna stand there, or you gonna dance, girl?" Ray MacCallister stepped in front of her, a cocky grin on his sun-tanned face. His black cowboy hat sat askew on his blond head. He eyed her hungrily, then licked his lips before he snatched her hand from Casey's and led her to the dance floor.

Ray was tall, and lanky, broad in the shoulders and ornery in the eyes. He had a habit of licking his lips every time he looked at her. Like a wolf over its prey.

Katherine had known Ray all her life. He was the only son from the neighboring ranch, and for the life of her, she couldn't figure out if she liked him or hated him. He could be a real ass or a real sweetheart, depending on his mood. Ray was definitely a looker and as sexy as the day is long, but there was always an edge to him she couldn't trust.

Katherine caught Casey's irritated glare now and then as Ray swung her around in time with the music. She felt bad but couldn't deny she liked the attention and the feeling of spinning in the arms of a confident man.

Her new boots clicked hard against the straw covered floor, and her skirt twirled a little too high, but it was fun. Fun! She couldn't remember the last time she'd had fun.

When the song changed to a slow country waltz, Katherine dropped Ray's hand and searched the darkened hall for Casey and the boys who, she discovered, had found their own girls to share dances.

"Oh, no you don't," Ray said. "We're gonna dance us a nice slow dance before you take off." He pulled Katherine close and pressed his body against hers.

"Back off, Ray," she warned. "You trying to get me killed? Momma'll have us both on the fire if these nice folks tell 'er you're pushing into me like that."

"Come on, honey. Your Momma ain't here. She won't find out. She could use a man of 'er own. Maybe then she wouldn't be such a cranky ol' bitch."

"Don't you dare call Momma that!" Irritation banged in Katherine's ears. Momma was strict and strong, but she was her flesh and blood. Katherine wouldn't tolerate someone talking bad about her even if what he said made some sense.

She yanked her hand away when he reached for it. "Back off. I'm done dancing with you." She pushed past him and walked to the lemonade bar, in desperate need of a cool drink to calm her nerves.

"One of these days, Kat. One of these days." Ray slowly walked toward his group of friends.

"Yeah, yeah." She waved him off. At least he'd been easy to shake, so maybe some other girl had caught his eye.

Peering over the glass of lemonade, she watched Casey and the boys flirt with some girls from school. All the same girls who shunned her and whispered behind her back in class. At a table next to them, Nancy Stevens, a girl she barely knew, shot daggers her way through her pale blue eyes.

When Casey saw the look of shock cross Katherine's face, he quickly came over.

"Why would she give me that look?" She pointed toward Nancy. "She doesn't even know me."

Casey laughed and shook his head. "You really live in your own world, don't you, Kat?"

"What do you mean?" She looked him square in the eye, not understanding.

"She's Ray's girl."

"Jesus, no wonder." Guilt nipped at her conscience. "Why'd he dance with me if he has a girl?"

Casey pulled off his hat and waved it in front of his face. "You *really* don't get it, do ya?"

"I guess I don't." She exhaled her frustration.

"There's not a guy in this place who wouldn't dump his girl to dance with you and every girl in here knows that." The blush that rose on his cheeks gave away his own feelings.

Katherine placed the glass on the barrel and took him by the hand. "Let's dance then."

On the dance floor, she placed Casey's free hand at the curve of her waist and stepped in close. She felt the quiver of his body through his fingertips. His palm instantly sweat through the silk band of her dress. He was nervous but she didn't care. She wanted to dance.

The world away from Ruby's Ranch was a mystery, but she knew how to the two-step like a pro. She wasn't about to squander more of her precious freedom worrying about Ray MacCallister, his jealous girlfriend or the other stares that followed her on to the dance floor.

They started off beat with an awkward stumble. Casey watched her feet, trying to match every step. Katherine stopped and squeezed his hand.

"Casey, look at me." She waited until he finally brought his embarrassed eyes to hers. "You don't dance with your feet, you dance with your heart. Feel the music bounce off the floor?" She repeated her father's instructions exactly as he'd said them to her all those years ago. "Just follow that rhythm and enjoy yourself."

He took a deep breath and relaxed when she flashed him a reassuring smile.

It felt so good to dance again even with Casey's clumsy steps. Memories of practicing with Daddy came flooding back to her. The father-daughter dance. A night she'd never forget. Dancing brought him back to her. There wasn't one thing that could ruin this moment for her, except knowing the clock grew ever closer to her ten o'clock curfew. The carriage was about to turn into the proverbial pumpkin.

"You know," Casey whispered in her ear, ". . . it's almost time to get you back. Your Momma'll fire me if I don't keep my word. God only knows what she'll do to you."

Katherine opened her mouth to agree, but she froze, her attention drawn over Casey's shoulder toward the door.

A masculine silhouette stood in the doorway, the moonlight from outside outlined his strong, athletic frame.

Her feet stilled even though the song played on.

Casey backed away to look at her.

She went quiet as everyone around her stomped and twirled.

Even as she sensed Casey's dismay, Katherine couldn't help but stare.

"What do we have here?" she whispered, unable to look away from the tall cowboy.

"I've never seen him before, but I have a feeling I'm gonna regret seeing 'im now," Casey grumbled as he stepped away to give her room to gawk.

Katherine studied the handsome stranger without a care she was being rude or forward.

He stood a good foot taller than her 5'4" inch frame. His short hair was the color of clay dirt under the brown, flat-brimmed cowboy hat. The snakeskin headband said a badass dwelled beneath. She chewed up the sight of him like he was one of Momma's gingerbread cookies.

His well-worn Wranglers were snug against his long, muscled legs and tight backside. His white, fitted shirt clung to his broad shoulders, a tuft of dark hair peeked out above the top snap.

He was older than her, maybe twenty-three or four, but she didn't care. She was eighteen now! What might have been illegal yesterday, were just some numbers tonight.

The large silver buckle at his waist looked like it could maybe be a roping trophy or the like, she couldn't really tell. It took everything she had not to walk over to get a better look.

The square-toed Frye boots were the most expensive thing about him other than the guitar he had slung over his back by a woven strap. He exuded class and restraint and some kind of pheromone that had her hypnotized.

Katherine hadn't realized she was holding her breath until Casey nudged her. "Come on, Kat. You look ridiculous. We've gotta go."

She ignored him and kept staring. She'd never been struck so by another person in her life.

The stranger's eyes, shadowed by the brim of his hat, now fixed on hers. They were dark and mysterious, obviously as curious about her as she was him.

"Oh, my," she whispered when he flashed a broad, playful smile. His closely trimmed goatee would surely tickle during a kiss. She prayed silently to feel that tickle in the very near future.

"*Oh my*, really?" Casey muttered, as he moved off the dance floor to gather his friends.

The lead singer of the band spoke out over the microphone. "I'd like to welcome Mr. John Lattrell to the stage. Come on up, John, and sit in."

Everyone, including Katherine, watched the handsome stranger walk toward the stage to join the band. He moved with a manly grace, telling her he'd be talented at anything he tried. Riding, dancing, lovemaking. Anything.

"Oh, my," she whispered again. She pushed her shoulders back when he headed toward her on his way to the stage. She regretted re-buttoning that top button.

She was stunned when their eyes met, like she'd been paralyzed by Blue Coral snake venom. He smiled again, obviously appreciating her reaction.

"I hope you're not leaving. You haven't even heard me play yet." His voice was deep and rhythmic. A sensual song without music.

Katherine didn't have words. She couldn't make her mouth move. She stared at him, smiling stupidly, wondering how his full lips would taste against hers.

"You all right, Miss?" He pushed the hat back on his head and leaned in for a closer look.

A low moan escaped when she caught the scent of his earthy cologne. His concerned gaze held her until the announcer again requested his presence on the stage.

"Miss?" He smiled again. "Are you gonna be okay?" He steadied her with a strong hand against the small of her back. She quivered from the heat of his touch.

When their eyes locked, a breath caught in Katherine's throat. The smile on his ruggedly handsome face, turned now to an expression of curious longing. The seconds that passed between them felt like hours. Just as he started to speak, Casey pressed his energy between them and broke the spell.

"She's fine," Casey interrupted, frustration evident in his tone. He grabbed her elbow and ushered her away. "And she's late getting home. Her *momma's* gonna give us hell if we don't get back home right now."

John held Katherine in his gaze as Casey and the boys escorted her out of the town hall. Her eyes stayed on him, memorizing his face, until she could see only his hand reaching for her through the open door.

Chapter 5

Katherine fell breathless against the cracked leather truck seat, her hand over her brow like a swooning maiden. "Wow, he's gorgeous and so mysterious." Her voice was a sigh.

"Seriously, Kat. Looks like nothin' more than a second-rate cowboy at best. Besides, he's too old for you. He could be a damn serial killer for all you know." Casey huffed, then hit his fists against the steering wheel in frustration.

So what if she swooned over John Lattrell? It wasn't like Casey owned her affections. Any more than Momma owned her goals and aspirations. "No, he's perrrrfect." She turned back to catch one last look, then leaned her head out the open window, letting her long auburn hair blow wildly in the summer breeze. Casey pulled the truck out onto the road, heading back to the ranch at a good clip.

The intensity that had emanated from the handsome cowboy's soulful, probing eyes made her quiver even now. She'd felt their connection. Where'd he come from? "Casey?" She bit her lip. "Why don't we go back? We hardly got a chance to dance."

Casey slammed on the brakes and hope leaped in her chest. But instead of turning around, he stopped the truck and looked at her. "Katherine. Can't you see he's not good enough for you?"

Her brow furrowed and the guys in the back of the truck fussed and knocked on the sides, irritated at being tossed around.

Casey reached over and ran the back of his hand along

her arm. "I mean it, Kat. You shouldn't be with him. You know I—"

Katherine put a finger to his lips. "Please don't say it."

Casey's jaw tensed, but he put the truck into gear and they sped down the road again.

She took a deep breath and gazed up at the sky.

The bright country stars were dulled by the silver-lined clouds covering the face of the moon. Dampness spread over the summer-burned pastures, making the wind cool against her hot skin. A hoot owl shrieked in the distance, warning the small rustling creatures of the night to beware.

"You're wrong, Kat. Wrong about him and wrong about me." Casey blew out a breath in defeat, then flipped on the radio to drown out her sighs. Waylon and Willie soothed her soul through the cracked dash speaker.

The hitch in Casey's voice brought Katherine back to reality. "I'm sorry. I didn't mean to hurt you."

She tried to wipe the dreamy smile off her face, but it wouldn't go away.

"Thank you for taking me to the dance. It means the world to me that you helped me get out of the house to celebrate my birthday."

He sniffed and shook his head again. "Yeah, that backfired on me, didn't it?" He glanced into the rearview mirror as the guys settled back in against the cab.

"I do love you, you know." She reached across the seat to touch his hand. "You're the best friend I've ever had."

"Friend," his voice broke. "That's just great." He looked down at her hand and squeezed it. "I'd always hoped to become more than a friend to you, Kat. Then some stranger shows up outta nowhere and you go gaga over him."

"I didn't mean for this to happen, it just did. I can't help it. I have no control over these things," she said, praying he would understand. "Besides, I'll probably never see him again anyway, so you're fussing over nothing."

When he looked back up, she caught his eye. She mouthed the words, "I'm sorry," meaning it with all her heart.

Casey blinked and pursed his lips. "I know I'm nothing special, Kat, but I've loved you since I set eyes on you." He slid his hand from hers and glanced toward the darkened road ahead.

"Please don't be upset with me. I can't stand it when you're mad," she whispered, wishing she had the kind of love for him that he wanted.

She could swear she saw a tear fall from the corner of his eye, but she'd never know for sure.

"You know I'm leaving Ruby's Ranch, Casey. That's been my plan all along. It wouldn't work between us. I need to go and you couldn't give up ranching. It's in your blood."

"You never even gave me a chance to make that decision," he bit back, his handsome, friendly face now riddled with despair.

Tears of regret bobbed in the corner of Katherine's almond eyes. The last thing in the world she wanted was to break her best friend's heart.

"What the hell?" Casey yelled out, his deep voice changed from disappointment to alarm when he jerked the wheel and locked the brakes.

As the truck started to spin out of control, Katherine caught a glimpse of a tall, strongly built man dressed in buckskin and feathers, standing in the middle of the road. The white paint on his dark face gleamed bright in the headlights. His jet-black hair hung in long braids on either side of his angular face. He didn't even flinch when he saw the truck careen toward him. He stood as still as a statue.

Katherine screamed when the fender scraped against the brush on the right side of the road, then skidded to an abrupt stop in MacCallister's irrigation ditch.

The guys in the back, used to riding atop bucking horses, jumped, uninjured, from the truck bed as the dust settled. Casey slumped dead still against the steering wheel.

A downed tree limb, lodged against the driver's side, blocked his door. The engine revved under Casey's heavy boot and mud from the ditch spewed in a semi-circle from the spinning tires. The eerie sound of the tinny radio echoing across the open field made Katherine shiver.

The smell of gas filled the cab in an instant. Katherine's heart sunk when she saw a line of bright red blood trickle down Casey's suntanned cheek. His hair, no longer captive in his hat, hid his face.

"Casey," Katherine screamed. "Casey, wake up? Oh god! We've gotta get out of here. Help, you guys!"

She could see the rise and fall of his short breaths but he didn't respond when she called his name.

Casey groaned in pain when she reached to touch his shoulder. "JB, we need to get 'im out of here. Now!"

"Hey man, you okay?" JB, Casey's best friend, reached in through the window and switched off the ignition. He lifted Casey's head gently from the steering wheel to assess the damage. "Ah, man," he said.

Casey groaned and leaned his head back on to the headrest, half conscious. JB worriedly glanced Katherine's way, then he pulled a clean white handkerchief from his back pocket and pressed it to the gash on Casey's forehead.

"Ahhh, nooooo," Casey moaned.

"Be careful. You've got yourself a fine cut there, brother, and it's bleedin' all over the damn place. Can't do anything half ass, can ya?" JB joked when he was nervous.

Casey gave no response.

"Help him, damnit!" Katherine grabbed Casey's arm and tried to pull him across the bench seat toward her, but he wouldn't budge, only groaned again in protest.

"I'm fine. I'm fine," Casey finally muttered, lifting his head drowsily, then laying it back against the headrest. "Make sure Kat's okay." He sounded like a sloppy drunk. When he reached to push his cowboy hat back away from the wound, he seemed perplexed it wasn't there.

Katherine's eyes blurred against the overhead light when the boys opened the passenger door and helped her out of the cab and up the muddy embankment. The smell of burned rubber, gasoline, and dust filled the air. A damp chill rose on her skin as shock moved in to protect her.

"Kat, you okay?" JB looked her over carefully. He moved the mess of auburn curls away from her pale face to check for injury. "Anything broken?"

She flinched each muscle and moved each limb to be sure. "I'm fine. I'm good." She shook him off when he tried to help her. "Please get Casey outta there. It reeks of gasoline."

"We'll get 'im, don't worry, Kat." He trotted off to help pry the branch away from the driver's side door.

It took a few minutes to clear her mind. But then she remembered. There was a man in the road. She walked back to where he stood.

"Hello, are you hurt?" she called out into the darkness.

No answer. He was gone. Disappeared. All that remained were skid marks from the tires, Casey's bloodied forehead, and a single owl feather that fluttered gently to the ground.

Katherine picked up the feather and twisted it between her fingers as she looked around once more.

An owl screeched overhead so loud, she gasped, then rushed back to the others. Another chill raised the hair on her neck.

"We need to get him to Doc," JB said, holding the handkerchief tight against the wound. "He passed out."

"Let's get him out of there." Another of the guys spoke up when the branch finally gave way.

JB and Dutch lifted Casey out of the cab and laid him gently on the ground with the bloody handkerchief still stuck to his forehead. Dutch pulled off his T-shirt and handed it to Katherine to use as a pillow.

"Casey?" She knelt and gently placed the T-shirt under his head. His eyes were half closed. His skin pale and clammy. His arms and legs sprawled awkwardly against the hard ground. When she moved the handkerchief away, the three-inch gash above his left eyebrow continued to bleed profusely, the skin around it already a dark bruise.

"Oh God, please wake up," she whispered, running her fingers through his sticky hair, pressing the cloth back to the wound. "Hang on, Casey."

She stood and hollered at the guys. "He needs help, now! Can we get the truck out of the ditch?" She prayed adrenaline would help the four of them move the truck back on to the road so they could get him to Doc.

JB jumped in behind the wheel, turned the key, and gunned the engine. The wheels only buried deeper into the damp ground. "Not budging, we're gonna need a tractor to pull it out."

"Turn the damn truck off, JB and get your skinny ass outta there," Dutch yelled. "It's leaking gas. Can't you smell it? Blowing us all up won't help Casey none."

"Someone's coming." Katherine pointed at the headlights approaching from the darkened road. "Dutch, flag 'em down before they run us over."

Ray MacCallister and his girl, Nancy, slowed the shiny new Ford not ten feet from the rear end of the ditched truck. "What's happened here?" he called out the window.

JB trotted over to speak to Ray. Though Katherine heard nothing of their conversation, she could see Nancy glaring at her from the passenger seat. Could she really think they were doing this to ruin her night out? Was she that insecure?

A second set of headlights rolled in and parked behind Ray's truck. Katherine recognized the driver the instant his long legs hopped over the short door of the vintage Jeep and made their way to where she stood protectively over Casey.

Their eyes met again. This time, his filled with concern and hers with gratitude.

"You all right, Miss? This don't look good. Is he okay?" He pointed to Casey sprawled on the ground. The singsong in his voice calmed Katherine instantly. He stepped closer to her and lifted her chin gently to survey her face for damage. "You all right?" he whispered, leaning intimately into her. Assessing.

She drowned in the depth of his eyes. "I'm not sure." For some unknown reason, she was on the verge of tears. He made her feel vulnerable and protected all at once and she barely knew his name.

"Honey, you might be in shock. You best sit down here and let me take a look at you."

"I'm fine." She squeaked the lie through her closing throat. The accident and the man had shaken her.

"You sure about that?" When he moved in to take her elbow, Ray grabbed him from behind and yanked him away from her.

"Who the hell are you? Kat don't need to be taking sympathy from some stranger. She's our girl. We'll take care of her. Why don't you take your pretty little guitar and your fancy Jeep and get on down the road?"

Katherine gasped at the gruff interruption. She wanted this gentle stranger to put his arms around her and comfort her. She wanted that more than any other thing in the world.

"Ray, stop," Katherine protested. She stepped between them. "Casey's hurt. We don't have time for this. He needs help now."

That didn't stop Ray from pushing. But her cowboy

didn't budge or raise a hand. He watched Ray cautiously, but Katherine detected a hint of amusement.

JB and Dutch crowded in and pushed them away from where Casey laid, still bleeding and unconscious. "Kat, Casey's not waking up." JB pulled her away.

"I gotta get Stan." She turned from the confrontation and ran toward home, knowing she would have hell to pay when she got there.

But Casey's health was more important.

She didn't look back to see what happened between Ray and her stranger.

She ran.

Chapter 6

Katherine slowed to a jog when she neared the house.

"Please, God, let me get to the barn without Momma seeing me," she mumbled to herself. A lecture was the last thing she needed.

The accident was not their fault, but somehow Momma would use it as proof she should never leave the ranch again.

Zeus and Zoë quietly moved in behind her as she slipped into the barn door and searched for Stan.

"Stan." Her voice was little more than a whisper, but it resounded loud against the quiet night. "Stan, are you in here?"

"Yes, I am, young lady. You need something?" Stan appeared from the far stall and walked toward her, his hands shiny from hoof conditioner. "Did you–?" He stopped the moment her face came under the light.

She gulped down panic. Tears bobbed in the corners of her eyes.

"What's happened, darlin? What's wrong?" He stepped in closer and watched the tears run down her cheeks.

"It's Casey. He's hurt." She ducked into his arms and accepted the hug he offered.

"Hurt? Where is he, honey? What happened?" He tossed the rag away and walked quickly toward the door.

Katherine followed close behind. "We were in an accident up the road. The truck went into MacCallister's ditch." She was breathless as she ran to keep up with his long strides.

"Accident? Are you okay?" He stopped to look her over.

"I'm fine, but Casey . . ." Her voice trailed off.

"I'm sure he'll be okay. Let's get the boys."

Stan yelled for the boys when they passed the bunkhouse. "Something's happened to Casey, let's go."

Katherine heard them get up and scramble into their boots.

Just when Katherine thought she'd succeeded in getting help without alarming Momma, Rube rode up astride her prized Appaloosa, Firefly.

"What's going on?" Momma looked from Stan to Katherine, then back again, sensing alarm.

"The truck's run off into the ditch, Rube. We're goin' out to check on Casey. He's hurt." His voice was calm, though Katherine could see his worry.

"Are you okay?" Rube slid down from the horse to get a closer look at her only daughter. "Are you hurt?" Her concern barely masked the irritation in her voice.

Katherine shied away from the stern look. "I'm fine, Momma, but Casey hit his head real hard. He's passed out and bleeding."

"We'll take care of Casey. You get in the house, young lady, and stay put. We'll talk about this later." Her tone was measured, as though she'd expected something bad to come of the dance. "You've had enough excitement for one day, don't you think? This is why I don't let you go out. It's too dangerous."

"It wasn't Casey's fault, Momma. There was a man standing in the middle of the road. He looked like a Native American, like a shaman maybe. He wouldn't move. Casey had to swerve to miss him." Katherine was desperate for Momma to understand it was an accident.

Stan glanced up quickly when he heard Katherine mention a shaman, but Momma shook her head at him in warning.

"A shaman? Really?" Momma failed to hide her surprise. "What do you know of shamans? Did you speak with this shaman and ask him what he was doing out on the road?"

"No, ma'am." Frustration flared. Momma was hiding something but Katherine didn't dare press her. "He was gone when I went back to look for him. Do you know who he is, Momma?"

This time Stan shook his head, more in wonderment than warning.

"Enough questions." Momma eyed Katherine, ignoring Stan. "Go to bed, young lady. We'll talk about this later."

Tension twisted in the air. Momma's worst fear came true, even if Katherine hated to admit it. Something did happen the minute she let down her guard. Katherine couldn't help but think Momma knew more than she was telling.

Katherine's heart sank. Even though Momma let her go out this evening, if Katherine stayed, she'd still be a prisoner on the ranch. No way would Momma let her go anywhere again after this.

But if she left in the morning, like she'd planned, would she ever hear how Casey was doing?

Would she ever get to see John Lattrell again? Would she get to feel the tickle of his goatee on her chin as they shared kisses?

Chapter 7

Katherine spent the night staring at the shadows marching across her bedroom ceiling. The packed suitcase seemed to call her. By morning though, the bag had changed its tune from enticing her to new adventures to mocking her for having no guts. She pulled the pillow over her head to block out the taunts.

She couldn't leave. Not with Casey injured, maybe permanently. And not with Stan and Momma sharing a secret about the shaman, but not telling her.

The Paint By Numbers kit Momma had given her for her birthday sat on her dresser. Another gift of appeasement, in hopes of fulfilling Katherine's need for culture from the outside world. As if the silly, juvenile painting of a tiger could ever substitute for the watercolors and pastels Daddy used to give her.

One day, and one day soon, even if it wasn't today, she would paint the Paris skyline. Maybe even sell her paintings along the sidewalk. Momma said it was a silly pipe dream, but Daddy had believed in her talent.

She longed to live amongst creative people. To see something other than cows and fields.

She finally gave up sleep and crept down the hallway, eager to hear about Casey.

Stan and Momma sat at the kitchen table, cups of coffee in front of each of them.

"How is he?" she asked.

"He's gonna be alright, honey." Stan's kind eyes comforted her.

Momma snorted. "He'll live, but he won't be doing any wrangling for a long while. Maybe ever." She stood and put her cup in the sink before striding out the back door.

Relief made Katherine stagger and she sank into the warm seat Momma just left. "Really, Stan? He's gonna be okay?"

He nodded. "Your momma's right, it'll be a long, slow recovery. He got himself a pretty bad concussion."

~ ~ ~

The next week flew by. Casey returned to the bunkhouse from the hospital. Momma and Stan were busy with the cattle, leaving Katherine to do all the cooking. Her bright spot was her painting. She lugged her old paint case around the ranch, sketching flowers and rolling hills, when she wasn't peeling potatoes or mixing cornbread.

Though Casey was doing better, he still suffered from terrible headaches and double vision from the accident. Those irritating symptoms kept him off his horse, which made things all the worse for a real cowboy who needed to be on the range to take a full breath. Doc warned him it could take weeks or even months for him to heal completely, but his disposition remained somber even when Katherine visited.

The heavenly smell of pot beans and ham hocks boiling on the gas stove wafted toward her when she stepped into the bunkhouse and handed him one of her paintings as a gift.

"What's this?" He squinted at the sloppy yellow orchids painted on the canvas. "Sorry, I can't make it out?"

She laughed. "It's a flower, not that you can really tell."

"Don't say that, Kat. It's cool you're painting."

This was definitely where men lived. Horse blankets and discarded chaps lay in the corner next to a pile of dirty cowboy boots. Large wooden chairs covered in rawhide lined the walls, with hunting and fishing magazines littering the coffee table. Floors of rough-planked oak shined brighter than she'd have expected for a bunch of ranch hands who spent most of their time tending their herd or grooming their horses.

Katherine loved the bunkhouse. It reminded her of Daddy, the roughest roughneck of them all, gone now for almost a decade.

Casey held the painting close to his face, trying to make out the detail. *Why did you give him a gift he needed to see to enjoy? What an inconsiderate idiot.*

"It's nothing really. I'm not very good. It's probably best you can't see it, anyhow." She took it from him and set it on a pile of magazines.

"I'm sure it's great, Kat." He was kind even though she sensed his sadness. She'd hurt him something awful. He was no longer the happy-go-lucky Casey she'd known and loved.

She sat next to him and worked to get comfortable in the oversized chair. It swallowed her, so she stuffed a pillow behind her back so she could touch her feet to the floor.

He chuckled in spite of his mood. "You okay there, Kat?"

"Shut up. Just because this place was built for giants." She laughed, then the room fell awkwardly silent.

"You know . . ." she finally said. "We haven't talked about what we saw out there on the road that night." Katherine reached for his hand, which he pulled away.

"Please don't," he said, melancholy again. "You confuse me when you touch me. I'm having a hard enough time keeping this all straight in my head."

Had she unknowingly led him on all this time? She was a hugger. It was her way. It never dawned on her he might take her affection a different way. Guilt made her squirm in the chair.

"What did you see?" she asked, changing the subject. "That night."

"It was so fast. Why didn't he move? Why wouldn't that stupid medicine man move out of the way?" His words came out rushed and loud. Hidden anger sparked in his eyes.

"He *did* look like a shaman, didn't he?" She felt vindicated. "I don't know why he didn't move," she said, working it over again in her mind.

Casey leaned toward her. "He just stared at us," he whispered.

"I went back to find him, you know. It was like he disappeared or something. All that was left was a feather."

Casey frowned at her, concerned. "You shouldn't have gone looking for him, Kat. I'm not so sure it was a good omen, him standing there, waiting to die."

"I feel like he was there for a purpose. To tell us something. I've been reading about shamans. Everything says if one appears to you, they're there to help you in some way." She prayed Casey wouldn't think she'd lost her mind.

He stood and walked to the window. "Why would he try to hurt us then? I mean, really. It's a pretty weird way to *help*." He didn't look back at her.

"Maybe he was there for me? How do you explain why I didn't get hurt at all in the accident?" She stood and followed him.

"I don't know anything about ghosts and spirits, Kat, but I do know if you go on like this in front of your momma, you may get locked up for good." He turned from staring out the window to look at her, blinking to clear the double vision.

"Wonder what's going on there?" She pointed through the window at Momma and Stan arguing in front of the barn door.

"Can't be sure, but something tells me they're discussing your shaman." He turned away. "You know, Kat, I'm thinking about leaving Ruby's Ranch when my head gets fixed."

Katherine froze. She prayed she'd misunderstood what he'd said.

"Did you hear me?" he asked.

She glanced once more at Momma and Stan, then took a deep breath. "Why?" She sucked in a breath. "Casey, you can't leave me here."

She knew it was selfish even as the words slipped past her lips.

"It's too hard to be here now, Kat. Now that I know how you really feel. I need to find my own life, my own future, with someone who can love me." He paused. "Like I love you." He settled back into the chair and leaned his face into his hands. "I can't take it. It's too hard." His eyes were red from rubbing against the double vision and from the ever-present tears of frustration and sadness.

"But I do love you, Casey. I'm so sorry, I just don't love you like that. Don't give up on me. Please don't go, Casey." Her eyes misted over as she knelt in front of him and placed her hands on his knees. He flinched with her touch.

He lifted his head and stared directly into her eyes. "I'll stay if you promise yourself to me, Kat. Only me. I can't stay here and watch you flirt with other men. It brings out the worst in me. It makes me lose control. I'm afraid I'd kill somebody." The look he gave her was sinister and threatening—a look she'd never before seen on Casey's kind face. Between the head injury and realizing she would never be his, he was at his wits end.

"Unless." He paused, hope lifting his expression. "Unless you want to come with me?"

Long moments passed between them as she ran the possibilities through her mind. A way to escape. But then, she knew it would be too cruel. "I'm so sorry, Casey," she whispered. "I can't go with you. As much as I want off this damned ranch, I can't take advantage of you like that, because I can't promise I'll ever love you like you want me to. I wish I could." Her voice disappeared in the air.

He said nothing but continued to stare at her in disbelief.

She stood and walked to the door. "Please don't leave without saying goodbye."

"I'll do what I have to do, Kat." His voice quivered.

Tears slid down her cheeks as she walked through the door, leaving her best friend alone to cry.

~ ~ ~

A week later, Casey was gone, leaving behind only a note. He wished her all the love and happiness in the world. She melted into a pool of regret when she read it. Yet another of those she loved left her alone at Ruby's Ranch to die and blow away like a tumbleweed rolling over the plains.

Guilt and loneliness threatened to drag her down. Augie held her so tightly, she could almost feel a physical embrace. He tried to soak up her desperation but it was too much for even him to take.

Since the accident, Momma rarely let her stray beyond the barn, not even to ride Cricket into the foothills to find her solace.

Momma hadn't talked to her about the shaman in the road as she'd promised. When Katherine brought up the subject, she was met with silence and a scowl, so she gave up. It wasn't worth upsetting Momma. *Someday*, Katherine thought to herself, *someday, you will have to explain this to me.*

Katherine wasn't allowed to hide in her room and feel sorry for herself either. Every day she worked alongside Momma tending the garden and preparing the meals for the ranch hands. Even in her haze, she learned the secret to Momma's gingerbread cookies and marveled at how beautiful and fun she could be when she wasn't being an overprotective bear.

They laughed and talked and cooked, and for the first time in her life, Katherine understood a little bit more about why Momma was the way she was. She was a woman left alone to take care of a ranch and a moody, daydreaming daughter. She wasn't an ogre all the time. She was doing the best she could. Until she felt threatened. Then the world would turn and the horns would come out again.

Chapter 8

Katherine marveled at the way the decades old blue willow china gleamed in the light as she wiped them dry. A gift to the newlyweds from her Grandma Adams before her young parents made the long, hot trek from the Oklahoma dustbowl to the Kern River Valley.

How brave they were, traveling all that way to face the unknown without the support of family. They'd done well for themselves even though Daddy's dream was cut short.

Ruby's Ranch was thriving, thanks to Momma. Katherine was proud, even as she wished each day for the perfect chance to get away. It was their dream not hers.

As she stacked the clean lunch plates into the freshly painted cabinet, she wondered what life would've been like had Daddy survived. Would Momma be more gentle or would she still be the overbearing rancher she'd become?

Katherine's heart beat double time as she headed up the hall. Her adventurer spirit was no different than her parents. Why couldn't Momma understand she, too, hungered to explore a world outside of what she'd always known? If anyone would understand, Momma should.

Katherine pulled out the suitcase again. It was time. Finally, after the years of longing, and these last weeks of waiting, there was nothing holding her back.

She dumped out all her cash to count it. Every penny she'd earned working the horses. Momma thought she'd spent it on paints. And she did buy some, but she mostly saved it. And she'd sold a few paintings at the gift shop in town to tourists eager to have a small piece of the American dream.

They had just finished lunch. She had one more afternoon and dinner to get through. She'd say good-night to Momma, but instead of climbing into bed, she'd climb out her window and start her new life.

Augie's attention diverted from her and Katherine raised her head. What changed?

She stood and moved to the bedroom window.

Dust swirled in the cool breeze as a single horse galloped fast up the driveway. This rider, she could tell, was comfortable in a saddle, though the horse seemed to be fighting a good battle. The rider reminded Katherine of Daddy, the way he carried himself high and strong, standing more in the stirrups than sitting in the saddle.

It couldn't be . . . could it? She tossed a quilt over the money spread out on her bed and dashed back to the kitchen.

"Who the hell is this riding up here like a bat outta hell?" Momma asked, irritation in her voice. She turned from the sink and set down the glass of water she'd filled. When the rider made no attempt to slow the horse's gait as he approached the house, she scowled. "A might full of himself, I'd say." She stepped out on to the porch to deal with this situation first hand.

Katherine knew better than to follow her out. Momma had sheltered her from strange men her whole life, but even more so since she started developing into a woman. Katherine was sure this time would be no different, so she leaned against the window sill to get a better look.

The majestic American Paint, at least fifteen hands high, was something to behold with large patches of black and white covering her muscled haunches. A black, diamond-shaped patch framed her face like the mask of Zorro. Her dark eyes were fierce and wild. Alive. Katherine saw herself in those eyes.

"Whoa, now," the cowboy called out as he reined in the mare with a gentle, steady hand. He was doing his best to avoid running straight through Momma's prized climbing roses growing around her morning porch. The skilled rider predicted every effort the mare made to unseat him.

"Ho," Momma yelled, with authority. The horse skidded to an abrupt stop not ten feet from where she stood. Momma moved to block the kitchen window. Katherine leaned down to watch the cowboy as he dropped to his feet in front of the porch.

She heard his voice first and goosebumps raised along her arms. "Pardon me, ma'am, I've just started working with her. I apologize for the bad behavior. I hoped she'd be settled before we made it here, but she's got spunk." His low, sultry singsong tone was like music to Katherine's ears. It was definitely the sexy cowboy from the dance, she could tell.

She bolted around to the fireplace room to eavesdrop through the half open front door. Zeus and Zoë sniffed and wagged their tails, threatening to blow her cover.

"Can I help you, young man?"

The authority in her voice straightened the man's shoulders and brought him to full attention.

Momma was known in these parts for her strong countenance, and her no-bullshit attitude. She held her own in a male dominated profession.

Katherine smothered her giggle when she saw the effect Momma had on him. He seemed so confidant and sure of himself the night they first met, but now he held back and remained respectful, obviously not immune to the spank of Momma's authority. *Oh, please don't let him be easily spooked.*

"Ah, yes, ma'am. My name is John Lattrell. Stan Blocker said you're in need of a wrangler? My specialty is breaking and training horses, but I can do it all." He flashed a disarming smile that had no effect whatsoever on Momma.

Katherine was another story. A shiver of heat ran over her when she saw the sexy smile she'd dreamt about a dozen times.

"Oh, my." A sigh slipped from her lips before she could stifle it, causing both John and Momma to glance toward the door.

Momma eyed him cautiously again. "I'm Rube Adams. This ranch is mine. Stan's my foreman." She pulled her hands up to rest on her hips and widened her stance slightly. She was trying to intimidate him, Katherine could tell, but he only smiled, petting the dogs who'd finally decided he was no threat.

"Yes, ma'am." He looked up at her again. "Mr. Blocker said you were the finest horsewoman he's ever seen." This time his smile was cautious, but hopeful all the same.

Katherine bent lower to witness this gorgeous cowboy work to singsong his way around Momma's protective guard. When she dropped her hands from her hips, Katherine knew he'd broken through, at least a tiny bit. The mention of Stan always softened her a little.

"Did he, now?" Momma reached for the door. "Well, that doesn't get you a job. What I've seen so far doesn't much impress me." She pointed toward the Paint who nibbled playfully at his shirt sleeve.

"Yes, ma'am." He held the mare's muzzle. "Stop it, girl. I'm trying to get a job here," he whispered to the horse, which made Katherine's heart skip a beat.

A smile broke across Momma's face for a second before giving him fair warning. "I'll give you a chance on Stan's recommendation, but you still have to earn your place here at Ruby's Ranch. Now take that crazy horse of yours to the back corral there and give 'er some water. I'll be out directly to watch you work."

Katherine moved as swift as a cat, slinking back into the kitchen, wiping down the counter, like she hadn't a care that the man of her dreams was leading his beautiful Paint back to her very own corral. *Please don't let my cheeks be as red as they feel.*

Without another word, Momma pushed against the door Katherine had been leaning against only a second before. "Get your boots on, young lady. We've got us a bronc to interview."

"A bronc, Momma?" she repeated innocently.

"Yeah, that's some kid Stan sent out here to apply for Casey's job."

"Oh, okay, I'll finish up when we come back in." Katherine was proud of how nonchalant she appeared. Shocked almost at how well she could hold it all in. Momma would throw him off the ranch in a hot second if she had a clue what was bubbling between her little girl and handsome John Lattrell.

Even though she screamed inside, Katherine kept her mouth shut tight as she followed Momma back toward the bedrooms to change into her riding gear. Yes, she definitely had a bronc to interview.

Chapter 9

Katherine spritzed herself with Jean Naté and wet her full pink lips with strawberry lip-gloss before heading out to the corrals. Hopefully Momma wouldn't notice she'd taken extra care with her makeup and slipped into last year's riding pants so they'd fit extra snug against her bottom. Her long auburn braid danced playfully between her perky breasts. The horseshoe buckle she'd won in a barrel race at the county fair gleamed bright below her flat stomach.

She was surprised and elated when Momma asked her to join, especially since this handsome stranger seemed by all accounts, absolutely perfect for any young woman to fancy and exactly the kind of man Momma would guard against.

Katherine walked two steps behind to hide her excitement. Momma's hair was pulled into the bun at the nape of her neck. Her favorite cowboy hat snugged down over her head. The long brown riding boots zipped nearly to her knees.

Momma was a handsome woman, still strong and shapely, even now. She must've been something to behold when she was young and full of love and promise. If God was kind to her, Katherine would look half as fetching in riding pants at Momma's age.

Katherine looked away when Stan met them on the path. No doubt he'd sense her excitement the moment their eyes met. She kept back and watched Stan and Momma together. Ahead, she caught a glimpse of John as he entered the round corral.

"I see you've been recruiting without me, Mr. Blocker?" Momma patted Stan familiarly on the back as he fell into stride.

Katherine stayed close enough to listen, hoping for an interesting morsel about John.

"We need a new hand with Casey gone, Rube. This young man comes with lots of experience and good references. He's worked horses since he was a boy. Grew up in Colorado and wrangled on some big ranches in Montana. Worked under Stew Handley out there in Butte these past few years. One of the best I've ever seen breaking ponies. If Handley says he's good, he's good."

Stan recited credentials like he was trying to sell Momma a vacuum cleaner.

"All right, all right." Momma smiled at Stan and held up a hand. "How'd you figure such a great cowboy might just happen into our little town then? Seems a bit far-fetched, don't you think?" She stared a hole through Stan, waiting for an explanation.

Katherine was more curious to hear this answer than Momma, though she acted as disinterested as she could manage. She looked off toward the ducks playing in the pond and perked an ear.

"Boy's brother is part of a little country band touring some in these parts. John's been following 'em around during the off season. Said he's lookin' for a warmer climate."

"California's certainly warmer than Montana, I'll give 'im that," Momma agreed, smiling back at Stan as she climbed through the fence to meet up with the young man and the agitated, half-wild stallion at the center of the corral.

Stan hesitated a few seconds, waiting for Momma to get out of earshot. When he turned to help Katherine steady herself on the top rail of the fence, he said, "Yeah, when I talked to John at the grocery, he mentioned he'd found a *few* things about our little town he really liked." He flashed a knowing grin then winked at Katherine.

She squirmed under the perceptive glint in Stan's bright blue eyes. He shook his head, then slipped his slightly bowed legs through the bars to join Momma and John.

Katherine beamed. Could *she* be the reason John stayed in town? She loved Stan Blocker. Thank God for him. She'd be completely crazy without him.

Katherine watched from the rail, as mesmerized by John as when she first saw him at the Sawgrass Dance. She hadn't expected him to remember a simple country girl with no life experience, but it was obvious by his smile, he remembered her.

She held her breath when he placed his dusty Frye boot into the stirrup and climbed on the back of the meanest young stallion on the ranch, his eyes trained directly on her. Buckshot had thrown every cowboy on the ranch more times than she could count. Momma threatened to sell him off to the MacCallisters if he couldn't be tamed.

Katherine prayed John could break him, so the beautiful animal *and* the handsome trainer could both stay on Ruby's Ranch where they belonged.

Buckshot was wild and nasty, but he was gorgeous, all shiny black and taut muscles. He looked more like a racing thoroughbred, standing some eighteen hands high, but he was just a well-formed quarter horse with infinite potential.

Momma traded a lot for him. She'd planned to breed him to her stable of brood mares to accommodate the growing ranch. That would all go away if he couldn't be ridden.

Katherine bit her strawberry-flavored lip, watching John settle his long leg over the top of the saddle, then tie his hand into the bronc rein.

Every voice around the pen went so quiet Katherine could hear the horse's breaths thread in anticipation. At first, both horse and rider stood dead still, evaluating one another. John talked to him, but she couldn't hear the words. Buckshot's ears perked back to listen. John seated his hat a little bit farther down on his head to keep it from flying off.

"Riding Buckshot's quite the test, Rube." Stan scolded Momma for setting John up to fail. "Try not to get hurt, son. We'd rather have you in one piece." He spoke quietly to avoid spooking the skittish horse.

John replied with a gentle, even tone. "We'll be just fine, sir. Won't we boy?"

"If he gets you down, roll out right away. He has a tendency to stomp," Stan warned.

Stan grabbed Momma by the shirttail and backed her away slowly toward the gate.

John acknowledged Stan with a tip of his hat. His eyes followed Katherine as Buckshot reared straight up, standing nearly vertical on his hind quarters. The powerful stallion did his best to knock the young, skilled wrangler off on his ass in one shot.

John clung to the angry animal like a spider to a wall. The fence shook when Buckshot's front hooves pawed angrily at the dirt. He jumped sideways trying his best to dislodge the clinging rider.

"What do we have here?" Katherine found herself so mesmerized, she hadn't even noticed Ray MacCallister and his father bellied up to the fence to watch the action. "Is that the guitar boy trying to break my horse? What a joke!"

Ray slipped through the bars, yelling and waving his hat, trying to spook Buckshot even more than he already was. "Get up, Buckshot. Knock that fancy musician off on his ass. Show 'em what you got. Don't let 'em get ya, boy."

Stan patted Katherine on the knee and pointed for her to move off the railing to safety. "Get back, honey. Make some room for this cock fight."

Katherine climbed down with her eyes glued on John. He easily held his own with Buckshot in spite of Ray's efforts to get him thrown.

"Ray," she scolded when he walked close, "you're gonna get 'im killed. Get outta there."

But Ray kept on, encouraged by his father's laughter.

Panic rose in Katherine's stomach as Buckshot jerked right, then left, kicked his hind legs out, and then reared straight up again.

John's expression stayed calm as he reasoned with the horse. His strong legs gripped hard against the slick sides of the leather. His body whipped to the rhythm of each buck.

He held his own and then some, even though Ray kept on, hoping to embarrass the new guy and win the horse.

Momma moved next to the senior MacCallister and whispered something into his ear. Katherine could tell by his surprised expression exactly what it was. When he laughed nervously, Momma grabbed his pinky finger and bent it back. She kept a steady smile on her face. His expression turned from playful to pain in a second's time.

It was hard to make out from where Katherine stood, but she thought she heard Momma say, "You get Ray outta there or no animal on this ranch will ever breed with yours as long as I live. You hear me, old man?"

Ray's father shook his head emphatically. "Yeah, yeah, sure Rube. Jesus. Calm down."

"Good. Smart man." She let go of his finger and looked around to be sure no one else heard. When she saw Katherine's shocked expression, Momma raised her eyebrow as if to say *this is how we deal with a bully*.

"It's all in good fun, Rube. Relax." Jacob MacCallister tried to lighten the mood, but she wasn't having it.

"Now," she said, frowning.

"All right, all right." He rolled his eyes. "Ray," he shouted, waving to his son, "get your ass outta that pen before Rube breaks my damn finger." He shook his hand to quell the pain.

Ray took less than a minute to crawl back through the fence and push past Katherine. "That pretty boy ain't gonna want you, anyhow. He'll get kicked off that horse and crawl outta here like a broken man."

Katherine pushed back against him. "You shut your mouth, Ray MacCallister. You don't know what you're talking about."

A low rumble from the crowd gathered around the pen made Katherine turn. Buckshot's gait had settled into a calm measured trot. His ears perked back to listen to John as he talked quietly to him and patted his sweaty wither.

"Well, would you look at that?" Katherine was amazed at how quickly Buckshot tamed. He didn't seem broken so much as respectful of his rider, like he trusted him more than feared him.

She crawled back up on to the rail to watch this handsome stranger conquer the roughest ride on the ranch without the use of a single spur or whip. She'd seen Buckshot throw the best of riders. John had managed a little wrangling miracle as far as she was concerned.

When John trotted by, he caught Katherine's eye and winked. Stan walked over and shook his head in warning.

"Be careful with this one, young lady. This ain't no boy you're toying with. He could break your heart."

Stan must've seen the wicked sparkle in her eyes. "Or maybe I should warn John to mind his own heart. That'd be more like it.

Chapter 10

Katherine stayed on the rail long after John climbed off Buckshot, led him to the trough for fresh water and wiped down the moisture and dirt from his coat. He glided his hands over the horse's long legs to make sure no damage was done during their first session together.

She marveled at how John's slow, gentle movements calmed the once fearsome stallion. In that short time, they'd become friends. Partners. Buckshot tucked his head demurely into John and listened as he spoke softly into his ear.

Where before the men feared to turn their back, Buckshot followed John into the barn without a lead.

"Hoo, boy," Katherine whispered, working her way down off the railing.

Stan came first out of the barn and sauntered to where the other horses milled around their feed.

"Hey, young lady, you still out here?" He waved for her to join him.

"Come help me brush out these mares. It's gettin' late." He handed her the shedding tool that hung from the fencepost.

Katherine kissed Cricket on the nose then moved the brush down her neck, running her other hand behind the brush to smooth down her coat. She was about to burst from the silence. She had so many questions.

"Stan, how'd he do it? Especially with Ray actin' a fool? How'd he stay on that horse?"

Stan peered at her over Cricket's back. "It's a gift. I've

seen horsemen like that before, but only a few times in my life." He kneeled to inspect the hooves for debris and cracks.

"I could watch him ride alllllll day longgggg." She breathed out a long breath and playfully fanned herself with the brush.

"Easy, darling." Stan stood back up and again shook his head in warning. "Be careful what you're thinking, Katherine Ann."

She looked down as a blush heated her face. "You know what I mean. Buckshot has taken you all down, but he-he broke him. Just like that." She looked up again with a shy smile.

"Not so sure Buckshot's exactly broken. More like he trusts John. I figure that horse belongs to 'im now whether Rube likes it or not. They're bonded."

Her eyes shot up with hope. "Think Momma'll hire him? Think she'll let him stay?"

Stan leaned toward Katherine. "She wouldn't hire the Pope if she knew you were this taken with 'im. You need to control yourself, young lady. Neither your Momma nor this boy needs to see all this here." He pointed at her love-struck expression. "It ain't proper to be this eager. Ain't ladylike at all. Your daddy wouldn't have it."

"Yes, sir." Katherine looked down again. He was right. Daddy wouldn't approve if he were here. "I'll try, Stan, but I'm pretty sure I'm in love. He's gorgeous, and mercy, now I've seen how he handles a wild animal, I'm all the more intrigued." She giggled, tormenting him.

Stan blew out a loud breath. "Oh mercy, you're something else. You're a smart girl, Kat. I know you'll do what you have to, to keep the peace 'round here. Remember your momma loves you. She'll do whatever she can to protect you from the evils of man. Especially the kind of evils you're looking to explore."

He patted Cricket on the rump, then walked toward the bunkhouse, wiping his hands on the seat of his well-worn Levi's. "Behave," he yelled back at her, then waved a hand.

Katherine watched until the bunkhouse door shut behind him and she wondered if she could get away with popping into the barn to introduce herself to John Lattrell before heading to the house to help with dinner. Would that be too forward? Stan wouldn't approve. It would have to wait for another time.

When she started toward the house, John's dreamy singsong voice called out after her, "Excuse me, Miss?" He trotted up and repeated his words, this time from directly behind her.

Zeus and Zoë wagged around him as Katherine, not sure what to do next, stood as still as she could manage.

"You going in so soon? I was hoping you'd come help me put Buckshot to bed." The sensuality in his voice sent vibrations of need through her in ways she'd never felt before. There's no way she misunderstood his feelings. No way he didn't want her as much as she wanted him. It was all there in the music of his tone. In the sensual energy he used to pull her in. She closed her eyes and waited until he spoke again, praying she hadn't dreamed it.

He came around to face her and took her hand. "We haven't formally met, I'm John. John Lattrell."

She kept her eyes closed a second longer, taking in his enticing cologne mixed with the scent of horses and leather. She took a deep breath in spite of Stan's warning. She couldn't help herself.

"Are you okay, Miss?" He cupped her hand between his and waited for her to respond. The warmth of his hands pulsed up her arm and over her entire body.

When she finally opened her eyes, he was so close she could see her own reflection in the deep blue of his eyes. Curiosity and confidence danced there. Soulful and wanting.

They asked a question of Katherine. A question she would always answer with yes.

"Do you have a name, beautiful?" He shook her hand once more. "Are you okay?"

Katherine kept her eyes trained on his, not able to answer until he moved his hand out of hers to touch her cheek. "Miss? Should I get someone?"

The thought of him running to the house to fetch Momma made her snap to right away. "Oh no, please don't. I'm-I'm sorry. I'm fine. I've never seen anyone—" She cut the sentence short. There was no way to finish the thought without sounding too forward or worse, too pathetic.

He waited again for her to finish but she fixated on the tiny dimples in his cheeks. His lips were full and curved into an ornery smile, the right shade of peach to make Katherine hunger for the summer-ripened fruit. His eyes were wise inside the guise of a young, confident man. His eyebrows danced when he talked.

She could tell he'd been around, but she didn't care. He was with her now, that's all that mattered.

John took a step back to look her over, obviously appreciating the effect he had on her. "Is this your ranch?"

She snapped back to reality. "I live here, but make no mistake, it's not my ranch. This place is one hundred percent Momma's. Her pride and joy," she answered abruptly, looking down to gather herself.

"I see." He pulled the hat from his head and ran his fingers through his short brown hair then settled it back down.

"I'm Katherine," she finally answered. "Katherine Adams. Some people call me Kat. You can if you'd like."

He looked relieved when she finally spoke. She nearly swooned when he placed a kiss on top of the hand she offered.

"Katherine, it is." He showed no interest in calling her by her nickname. "Very pleased to meet you." His hand was gentle and rough at the same time. She held tight to the warmth and energy. Not a hint of nervous sweat, whatsoever.

"You were amazing with Buckshot. I—I've never seen anything like that."

He pulled his hand from hers and stuck it in his pocket. His cheeks blushed and his eyes darted away from hers. Embarrassed. "Buckshot's a good boy. Just needed someone to listen to him is all."

"*Listen* to him?" She waited for John to meet her gaze once again.

"Most creatures want little more than respect and for someone to really listen to 'em. Horses are no different." He smiled, almost as if he knew this was the one thing Katherine had craved her entire life—for someone to truly listen to her and to really understand.

Maybe she'd finally found her someone.

Chapter 11

Katherine nearly floated the rest of the evening, proud she'd finally gained the courage to actually speak to John and excited he seemed as taken with her as she was with him. Even more excited at the prospect of him staying on the ranch for good.

She was so enraptured she barely noticed the savory bites of chicken fried steak and mashed potatoes which usually held her complete attention. Even Momma's famous biscuits and gravy didn't bring her back to the present.

John was staying. He'd be on the ranch where she could see him. Her fork froze on its journey to her mouth. John was staying. But . . . she'd planned to leave. Tonight! Her packed suitcase and her money waited in her room.

"Katherine!"

She jumped and realized Momma had asked her a question. Twice.

"I'm sorry, I was thinking about something else. Yes, Momma?"

Momma gave her an assessing look and if Katherine didn't know better, she'd swear Momma just read her mind.

But all Momma said was, "Don't forget to put the cast iron into the oven to dry so it doesn't rust."

"I won't," she said and returned to her thoughts as she stood and carried the dirty dishes to the counter.

Leave? How could she leave now? John felt like her destiny. She needed to see it through. She squirted soap into the thin stream of hot water falling into the sink. Momma and Stan kept up a quiet discussion at the table behind her.

She'd watched John climb on the beautiful Paint and ride out the long drive he'd galloped up earlier. He was no longer a stranger to her, but the man she'd marry. There was no doubt in her mind. She'd figure out how to make that happen without Momma derailing her plans. She had to. But there would be no midnight flight from Ruby's Ranch tonight. For the first time, leaving the ranch was the last thing she wanted to do.

The dishes were washed and dried and stacked while Katherine's thoughts kept circling back to John.

When she heard his name, Katherine perked an ear. She listened intently as Stan and Momma bantered on about when *the boy* could start, and what *the boy* would do first, without giving a care of the wicked answers she had rolling around in her own mind. Momma was so focused on *the boy* as a new ranch hand, she never gave a thought that *the man* had already won her daughter's heart.

Stan was a different story. He glared caution at Katherine now and then, which kept her giddy smile in check. He needn't worry. She'd never sabotage this. John Lattrell was Momma's best chance at keeping her little girl on this ranch. Katherine wouldn't hesitate to use that trump card if Momma even batted an eye.

With the dishes done, Katherine left them to continue their planning and made her way to the bathtub for a nice warm soak before bed. She did her best thinking in the tub. The layer of lavender bubbles tickled her skin when she stepped into the water. The delicious fragrance relaxed her mind and her body.

Up until today, every bath filled her mind with thoughts of bright neon lights and loud honking horns. Cities alive with interesting people. The excitement of the theatre and the fancy clothes and elegance of runway models. Gallery openings and shows. Maybe her paintings on the walls. Every other bath until this one, that is.

This one was filled with thoughts of John. The way his shapely rear end sat so strong and natural in the saddle. The respectful command he had over Buckshot. The seductive, patient way he watched as she struggled for words. The dreamy singsong of his deep, sensual voice. He'd brought out feelings and needs she never knew existed. Delicious, aching feelings.

When she let out a sigh, the bubbles sizzled and popped. She glided the bar of jasmine soap up her taut stomach, then over her tender breasts, concentrating there for a long moment. *Katherine Lattrell. Mrs*. John Lattrell. It did have a ring to it.

~ ~ ~

Just when Katherine was sure she'd never fall asleep for thinking of John, she was caught up in a disturbing dream. The shaman was in the headlights again. This time, his hands were raised above his head as if reaching for the stars. The squeal of the tires against the dirty asphalt matched the screech of the owl that fluttered away from where the shaman stood. He was gone again. Leaving smoke instead of flesh.

The pink, cotton nightshirt clung to Katherine's sweaty body. Her hair, now too hot around her face, made her squirm in the sheets.

Katherine's eyes opened wide as a breeze from the open window hit her damp face. The smell of rawhide and Momma's climbing roses danced in the air. The quiet rustle of her faithful dogs settling down on the porch was all she heard until an indistinguishable sound, ever so faint, came from the darkness inside her room.

At first there was only mist hanging in the air. She blinked against the vision of a shadowy figure as it formed at the foot of the bed. She held her breath to halt any sound.

It was light more than substance. The body floated in waves rather than holding solid. She was instantly soothed by the presence, yet still unsure she'd awakened from her dream.

The face was that of an elderly man, with sharp, regal features. His hair, long and gray, hung down in front of his shoulders. He was tall, but bent with age, gentle and unthreatening though he didn't smile. He wore a Native American cloak of bright orange, cobalt-blue and red beads woven into soft, tanned rawhide. Leather fringe hung freely from the sleeves.

He propped his crooked body up with a carved wooden walking stick, an owl head made of stone in the palm of his hand. A string of feathers braided into a leather strap dangled from the handle.

This was not the same man from the road, Katherine was sure of it. But this was no coincidence either. Something or someone was trying to tell her something. But what? Her life was simple and boring, no danger lurked. What could they want? All she could do was wait and watch.

He said nothing but she heard him as though he had. "Beware, child." The words came loud and clear into her mind.

"Beware? Beware of what?" She had no idea what his message meant or what she was expected to do, so she laid as still as a child pretending to sleep.

He took one wary step closer. The feathers on his walking stick waved in the same breeze that cooled her damp skin. It wasn't a dream and she knew it, but if she moved it would become too real and she'd have to scream. It would be the natural thing to do.

"Beware, child!" The wind brought the warning a second time.

"I don't understand," she whispered back. She blinked to keep him clear in her sight.

He glanced out her window and gazed over the moonlit

pasture, then looked back again to her. He said nothing more, only watched her.

Katherine didn't know whether to get out of bed and run or try to reach for him, so she stared back, desperate to understand his message.

A moment later, she woke again. Seven o'clock, and she was alone like every other morning. No signs of her visitor lingered.

Three lime-green and pink hummingbirds fought over the red-tinted sugar water hanging outside her window. Fearless, they buzzed at each other like kamikazes when one attempted to drink. The morning sun shed bright orange and yellow light over the seeding fields. The wranglers, including John, were already out moving the cattle grazing outside the corrals. Katherine felt the ground shake under their heavy hooves.

She sat upright and lifted the comforter to her chin. She couldn't get her mind around what had happened. Had she dreamt it? Was she going crazy? Or was it really a message she should heed?

She reached for the glass of water sitting on the bedside table, then froze, her hand hovering. A second owl feather sat next to the one she'd found in the road the night of the accident.

It was real. Did she have Native American spirits trying to tell her something important? Or was it something sinister? That was the question. Somehow she knew Momma had the answer.

Chapter 12

The end of summer barbeque at MacCallister Acres was a tradition every rancher within a hundred miles looked forward to, even though there was plenty of work still to be done. Their work was never finished, but the annual event was not to be missed.

This gathering gave ranchers an opportunity for some real bargaining, something essential to the trade in the Kern River Valley. Deals were made for breeding as well as horse, cattle, and service trading of all kind. It also gave their egos a chance to stack their herds against the local competition. Everyone always attended.

Two prime hogs and one fatted steer were donated by the local cattle association to help feed the hungry ranchers and their families. A bounty of fresh corn on the cob, garden-grown green beans, cowboy potatoes, and pot beans laid out next to sheets of thin, crispy cornbread made every mouth water. Giant vats of sweet tea, and a half-dozen kegs of iced cold beer sat ready to quench the crowd's thirst. A line of pans filled with Margie MacCallister's homemade peach cobbler, still steaming from the oven, sat covered at the far end of the table waiting to be paired with the tubs of homemade ice cream in the buckets below.

The MacCallisters knew how to throw a party, there was no doubt about that. And Katherine relished every chance she had to get dressed up. To see other people besides the hands at Ruby's Ranch and to let them see her. It was one of the rare occasions Momma was distracted enough to let her be. It was a welcome change from her constant worry about the message she'd been given by her haunting dream.

Katherine wore her favorite pale blue peasant dress, the top button open and showing the gold dreamcatcher necklace Daddy had given her before he died. Her auburn hair was curled in wide ringlets down her back, the long bangs pulled away from her lightly painted face by a large tortoiseshell clip. Though she would've preferred five-inch heels to complete the look, she wore the finely-stitched leather cowboy boots instead. More to keep the peace than for the love of the look. She'd learned to pick her battles.

When she walked into the backyard fortress, she found herself overtaken by the revelry of the younger generation doing their best to beat one another in a game of horseshoes. Their parents, much more subdued, wandered around the huge covered patio, cups of beer in every hand.

The women, minus Momma, marveled at the expanse of Margie's garden, and the beauty of the bright pink trumpet vines dangling from the patio trellis. A three-piece band, made up of an acoustic guitar, a fiddle, and a harmonica, played down-home country music in the background. She recognized them right away as the band John had joined at the Sawgrass Dance. It was obvious by his broad shoulders and angular jawline that the fiddle player was his brother.

Katherine watched from the entryway for a while, unsure of where she wanted to start. Did she want to grab a glass of sweet tea so she had something to hold, or did she want to shadow Momma, to watch her bargain with second and third generation saddle-worn cowboys wearing their western finest?

"Go on, girl." Stan nudged Katherine toward the crowd of teenagers. "Here's your chance to mingle. You're always begging your momma to get out. Well, you're out. Don't waste time spying on 'em." Stan gave her an encouraging smile, then walked ahead to catch up with Momma, already knee-deep in breeding negotiations for her lot of two-year-old heifers.

Katherine opted to grab the drink first, hungry for interaction but still unsure and timid. She spied all the treats as she walked along the table. She got in line at the drink table to wait her turn.

"You want me to sneak you a beer, Kat?" Ray walked up from behind and pressed his body against hers.

She stepped forward, away from him, hoping no one saw. "Ray, why are you always trying to get me into trouble?" She looked around for Momma.

To her surprise, he moved away and smiled. "Sorry, Kat. Just messing with you."

It took a second to process he was being nice.

"Why don't you come over and play some horseshoes with us when you're done? Everybody's over there." He seemed sincere rather than his usual obnoxious self.

"Thanks, maybe I will." She smiled, relieved. She grabbed a cup, then turned to watch as he trotted toward the kids around the pit.

She took a seat along the side of the pit so she could watch the guys show off their skills. What an odd game. The goal was to wrap a steel horseshoe around an iron stake in the sand.

Ray gave Katherine a cocky grin each time an opponent fell.

Soon, she was having fun again.

"You wanna try?" Ray startled Katherine with the question as he waved for her to join him behind the line. "Come on, it's easy."

She looked to see Momma and Stan sitting around the fire pit with the elder MacCallister and two other middle-aged men she recognized from town.

Did she dare? Why not? It was a game. What could it hurt?

She placed her glass of sweet tea on the table then walked over and accepted the set of horseshoes to toss.

"Put one of those beautiful feet in front of the other, and use the opposite hand to throw. Keep your hand flat, like this." Ray held out his arm as if he was tossing a softball underhand. "Then, let it go."

Katherine barely noticed him behind her, guiding her hand through the throw.

"Like this?" she asked, letting go of the shoe. It landed a good five feet short of the target but was dead on line.

"A little more umph and you'd had yourself a ringer." His mouth was so close, his breath tickled against her ear.

Katherine jerked away. "Ray, keep your distance."

Nancy glared at them from alongside the sand pit. The crowd of teens bent their heads together to share a whisper.

She drew a deep breath and ignored them. She was just having some innocent fun, learning a new game, playing with an old family friend.

The second shoe she threw ricocheted off the stake with a loud clang and landed near a pair of familiar, dusty Frye boots.

Katherine slid her eyes up the long legs, and over the stiffened body, finally settling on John's questioning face. His expression was not playful like the last time she'd seen him, but a mix of concern and jealousy.

"Oh, I, I, ah, better let you have this." She turned to hand the remaining horseshoe to Ray and get away from him as fast as she could. She didn't want John to think there was anything going on between her and Ray MacCallister.

"Oh, no-no-no, you're not goin´ nowhere. We need to have us a little contest. Let's say you and me against the music man there, and the lady of his choice." Ray said it loud enough for everyone to hear.

The crowd hushed when John strode to Nancy and took her by the hand.

"I believe this young lady here and I can take you." His singsong voice was serious now, barely masking the threat.

Nancy looked frightened. She glanced from Ray to John and back again as if asking permission.

"Seems fair," Ray agreed. He tossed the remaining shoe toward the other side of the sand pit, missing them by mere inches. "Let's do this thing. We'll even let you go first."

Katherine stared at the two men. The last thing she wanted was to compete against John, especially with Ray. When John cuddled in a private whisper with Nancy, a twinge of jealousy nearly paralyzed Katherine.

Ray leaned in to give her instructions.

"We can't let 'em beat us, Kat. You ready for this?"

A streak of competitiveness ran through her veins when John leaned into Nancy again, sharing a secret that made her blush.

"Don't you worry," Katherine said through clenched teeth. "We won't lose because of me."

Ray gripped her elbow and pulled her to look at him. "I'm going to pitch from the other end. I'll send Nancy to this side. Don't forget whose team you're on." He stomped away and jerked his thumb over his shoulder. "Nancy, you move to the other side."

She scuttled toward Katherine, still glaring.

Katherine ignored her opponent and concentrated on the feel of the heavy, cold iron in her hand.

John threw a ringer first try, his concentration as steely as if he was atop a bronc. The second leaned against the stake. He glanced over at Ray and tipped his hat, challenging him to do his best.

"Don't worry, Kat. I got this." Ray moved his hat back on his head and picked up the shoes. He positioned himself, then made his first toss. The throw swung twice around the rod and settled in for the ringer. "Now we're talking." The second shoe hit the ground a foot in front of the goal, then tumbled into the rod for a second ringer.

"You can't beat that," he yelled out. John seemed unfazed.

"Go ahead there, Nancy, show 'em what you got." John smiled an adoring smile at the blushing girl, which sent a lightning bolt of frustration through Katherine.

"Don't worry, honey. We've got this," Ray assured her from the other side of the pit.

Nancy's first attempt barely made it halfway to the target.

John called to her when she seemed to cave into herself in embarrassment. "Don't worry about them, honey. Just throw that thing as hard as you can." He glanced at Katherine and chuckled at her sour expression.

She wiped the frown from her face. She knew exactly what he was doing now, and she didn't like it one bit. But two could play at that game.

"I'm not worried, Ray. Not even a little." She gave him a wicked smile. "Come on, Nancy," Katherine urged. "Ray would love for you to beat 'im."

Katherine was no fool. She'd spent the majority of her life working around Momma. If the boys could taunt one another, then so could the girls.

Nancy looked at her with distain. She said nothing, too polite to be unladylike. But Katherine could see frustration bloom.

Katherine winked at John when he looked up, proud of herself for causing Nancy to fluster.

"Never mind her, darling. Just put that little shoe around that there stake. Pretend like these two aren't even here. It's just you and me." He purred the words.

John's tender tone did Katherine in. As much as she'd hoped to torment him, John was better at this game. She was not mad as much as intrigued by the power he had over her. His little show only made Katherine want him more.

Nancy's next throw landed an inch from the rod. Katherine could see her confidence swell.

"Nice," John said. "Very nice."

Nancy blossomed into a different girl under his compliment. Her eyes sparkled. She stood up straight for the first time. Shoulders back, breasts out. The denim dress she wore seemed to fit better against her generous curves.

Katherine knew the last throw would be a ringer before it ever left her hand. And it was.

"Your turn, *Kat*." Nancy growled the words more than spoke them. "It's all up to you now. No pressure."

Katherine gulped when she noticed not only had the younger crowd grown quiet and watchful, but most of the adults now lined the pit as well. To her dismay, Momma watched intently, a frown on her face.

There would be no victory for Katherine tonight, even if she tossed two ringers. Too much attention and too much testosterone was the kind of equation that grounded Katherine every time.

Her heart fell when Momma headed toward her. She knew the look. Public humiliation was sure to follow.

"Yes, ma'am," she said before Momma spoke a word. Katherine ducked her head down as she passed by the curious onlookers, unwilling to even catch John's eye as she was quickly escorted from the barbeque. She couldn't catch a break.

Chapter 13

Katherine kept her head down for the next few days, thankful Momma avoided her as well. She knew when the talk came, it would be a hard one. She'd been through it a million times. She'd survive this one like all the others.

John kept himself scarce as well. Aside from the seductive, far away strumming of his guitar that called her name in the quiet of evening and the occasional glimpse of him riding Buckshot out in the pasture, he'd all but disappeared. As much as she wanted to crawl out of her window and find him, she knew better. Momma would surely get rid of him if they were caught.

Katherine sipped the last of her tea before starting the breakfast dishes. What was she still doing here? If the point of staying had been to find out Momma's secrets about the shaman in the road and to get John's attention, maybe she should leave now. Neither goal seemed attainable.

The smell of breakfast bacon permeated the air long after the meal was done.

After the dishes, Katherine whipped up a couple dozen of the family gingerbread cookie recipe, trying to clear the smell of fried pork and hopefully, make peace. It was inevitable she'd be banned from doing anything fun for the foreseeable future so all she could hope for was permission to ride Cricket away from the torturous silence.

After the cookies were done, Katherine set up her paints and sketched a vase of daisies on a red gingham table cloth. Momma interrupted her as she considered the right shade of yellow for the daisies. Mustardy or more lemon?

"I want you to mix up a few large pans of meatloaf for dinner, and get a sack of potatoes peeled and cut," Momma said as she strapped her apron on and laid out the iron skillets.

"Yes, ma'am." Katherine continued to paint with her eyes down.

"We've hired that cocky cowboy, John Lattrell, and we're gonna have us a little welcome dinner, Ruby's Ranch style." She kept her eyes on Katherine.

Katherine blinked rapidly, but otherwise managed to keep her face expressionless. "Yes, ma'am, I'll get dinner started." The corners of her mouth didn't even curve.

There was a God.

Katherine propped the small canvas against the back of the hutch and put away her supplies before starting the meatloaves.

She worked and waited, expecting Momma to bring up the other night, but she continued to talk about dinner instead.

"Bring in a mess of beans too. The boys'll be joining us. I'll make the cornbread when I come in from my ride."

"Ride? If I mix up the cornbread, do you think I could come along?" Katherine made her first attempt to meet Momma's gaze.

She looked so exhausted and irritated, Katherine felt a twinge of guilt.

"Cricket could use a little workout. We haven't been out in a while."

Momma pulled dishes down from the cabinet, then lined up the mason jars on the counter. She steeped a handful of tea bags in a pitcher of water and set it in the window sill to brew in the sun.

"I suppose that'd be all right," she agreed. "But we're still gonna have a talk."

Katherine's heart sank. She was so close. At least she'd thought so.

"Yes, ma'am," she whispered. Her eyes dropped down to the bowl of ground meat and eggs and cracker crumbs.

Momma clanged the silverware into the plates, then headed to set the table with the stack of Blue Willow in her arms. "Yes, ma'am, indeed."

Katherine's stomach lurched when Momma brushed past her. The anticipation of getting yelled at was far worse than the confrontation.

She gathered every ounce of courage she could muster and followed into the dining room. She watched Momma place one setting in front of each of the ten chairs at the long oak table.

"Momma?" she asked quietly, unsure why she was about to say what she was about to say. "If you don't mind, I'd prefer to talk about this now, rather than waiting." She exhaled a breath, thankful to get the words out before she lost her nerve.

Momma paused a moment before setting the last plate in place. Then she sat.

Katherine saw Momma's irritation rise with the redness of her face, then just as quickly, fade.

"All right, young lady." She patted the table for her to sit. "Let's have our talk now then." She peered directly into Katherine's soul.

"Yes, ma'am. Thank you." Katherine did her level best to hide her fear. She curved her body uncomfortably into the dining chair across the table to keep a safe distance away.

"So, since you're so eager to have this talk, what do you suppose made me so upset the other night? Do you even know?"

Katherine gathered herself. "I don't, Momma. I really don't." Her entire body tensed.

"You don't know, huh? Don't you see how men look at you? And the women? They don't want you around their men." She thrummed her fingers against the table. The bun at the base of her skull tightened as she spoke. Her frame, though small and delicate, was as intimidating as a tornado.

Katherine squeezed back against the chair and crossed her slender arms across her chest, thankful Augie had surrounded her in his cocoon.

"I was playing horseshoes, Momma. I wasn't trying to attract attention." Her eyes filled with tears.

"Well, that's the problem, Katherine Ann. You need to pay attention to how you affect people around you. You flit when you walk, and you push your breasts out like you're begging for them to be seen. Keep yourself buttoned up, young lady, and pay attention when these men flirt. They want one thing, and I don't plan for you to give that away anytime soon."

Katherine kept her eyes down as Momma ranted on. There was no sense in trying to explain that she just wanted friends, someone to talk to and laugh with. Someone to love. Momma would never understand, even though she and Daddy were already in love, with plans to marry, by the time they were her age.

"Yes, Momma." Katherine looked up. A tear slid down her cheek. "I'm sorry. I promise, I didn't mean to . . ." And she lost her words.

Momma gave her one more second to finish, then huffed as she got up from the table. "Go finish preparing the food for dinner like I told you, then take your mare for a ride. Dry those eyes, redirect your energy to your own growth, and realize you don't need a man to accomplish things in life. Take pride in yourself." She stood. "Go on." Momma shooed Katherine out of the chair toward the kitchen.

She was gone to the stables and Katherine was back in her own silent hell, wondering if tonight was the night she should make her escape.

Chapter 14

Katherine found calmness riding her beautiful mare away from the corral. Cricket was the best friend she'd ever had. Non-judgmental and ever loyal. Her stride was long and balanced, perfectly timed and smooth. She listened patiently as Katherine cried. Aside from Stan, Cricket would be the only creature on this bloody ranch she'd really miss when she was gone.

The afternoon breeze dried the tears she'd shed while listening to Momma go on. She'd barely even kissed a boy, much less what Momma was suggesting. At this rate, she may never find someone to love, and if she did, Momma would surely run 'im off.

The dying purple lupines that grew wild over the range crunched under Cricket's hooves as Katherine led her into the foothills above the ranch. Haley's Peak, now a good distance behind her, was a fair amount breezier than down in the valley. The wind felt good against her face. Cleansing.

A large red tail hawk swooped in front of Cricket, picking up a fat field mouse for a snack. Woodpeckers squawked as she neared their nesting trees.

Katherine slowed Cricket's pace to gaze back over the ranch in the distance. How beautiful and serene a picture it made. How could such a postcard setting be so stifling?

Even though it was home to her, the ranch, and her over protective mother sometimes felt like a plastic bag tied over her head. No shimmering lights, no excitement, no culture, nothing she envisioned for her future.

She wanted to remember it just like this so she pulled out her sketch pad and penciled in the little house in the distance and the red and white barn with corrals of milling horses. The dots on her picture represented a hundred head of cattle grazing in the high corral. The large vegetable garden next to the house drawn as starred pencil marks all in perfectly straight rows.

It was impressive, Ruby's Ranch, but it wasn't her paradise. Someday, New York, Los Angeles or even Paris. She'd find a way. Paint brushes in hand along the artist's boulevard. The gondolas slipping by on the glassy Seine. The scent of fresh baked French bread and dry red wine in the air. The thought of exploring a world so very different than her own brought a hopeful smile to her lips.

Katherine replaced the sketch pad in her saddle pack and continued her ride. They took the rocky path past the top grazing land, past the ridgeline fences.

"Let's go up, girl." She spoke quietly to the horse who perked her ears back to listen. "You take me where you wanna go this time." Katherine twisted the reins loosely around the saddle horn and laid forward across Cricket's withers to rest.

The horse didn't miss a step. She carried her cargo gently beyond the last foothill to the rock formations atop Mount Sierra.

Katherine closed her eyes and held tight to the warmth and security she offered. The scent of well-groomed horse and saddle soap soothed her frayed nerves. Cricket felt like a gentle swing beneath her, rocking her to and fro, until the ache Momma had planted faded away.

How would Momma ever understand when Katherine left the ranch?

Katherine laid against her faithful horse for so long she barely noticed when the summer burnt flowers under the horse's hooves changed to mossy green clover. The sun, now a good bit lower in the sky, bled bright yellow rays of light from behind a single cloud.

When she sat up, she found Cricket had led her to a place she'd never seen in all her years of riding these hills. A mountain creek tumbling into crevices along the ground was loud against the quiet breeze sifting through the leaves. Sweet jasmine hid coyly in a blanket of orange and green poison oak. The trees and brush were tall and full, bringing shadows over the ground so different than the sun-drenched open plains around the ranch.

"Whoa, girl," she murmured, mesmerized by the mystical meadow. "Where've you brought me?" She looked back over her shoulder from where they'd come and recognized nothing. It was as if they'd been transported somewhere completely new.

Katherine's heart thumped with excitement and fear. Her first thought went to Momma who would be out of her mind with worry over her daughter's irresponsibility. But that faded quickly when she allowed herself to soak in the calmness of her surroundings. Cricket brought her to a whole new world.

The gentle mare bent to nibble the delicate grass at her feet as Katherine kicked her leg over the saddle and slid to the ground. "How did I not know about this place? I wonder if anyone else has been up here."

Katherine took a few steps toward the ragged rock formations, careful to avoid the sticky leaves of the poison oak. Morning glory vines twined through tall live oak trees, the bright purple flowers opened wide where the sun touched them but hung shriveled in the shade. The deep brownish-red of the Manzanita bark gleamed from a recent rain. Low-lying fern and clumps of orange poppies covered the ground at the base of the rocks.

The temperature was a good ten degrees cooler within this natural fortress. Birds bounced cheerfully at the tree tops, ground squirrels leapt from rock to rock, then into low lying branches to watch Katherine as she explored.

A few steps further into the brush, Katherine spotted Firefly grazing on the far side of a large clearing. She ducked quickly behind a tree when Momma walked into a circle outlined with smooth bowling ball size rocks.

"What the devil?" Katherine whispered.

Larger rocks etched with signs of Earth, fire, water, and wind stood at the north, south, east, and west points of the circle. The smaller rocks were laid out like spokes on a wagon wheel. An impressive boulder with a huge sun etched into the granite stood sentry in the center.

Momma touched each sign as she walked the perimeter of the circle. Katherine held her breath when Momma faced the tree she hid behind, then exhaled in relief as Momma turned back toward the middle of the circle. When she reached the center and touched the sun, something large moved the branches behind Katherine.

Chapter 15

"Who's there?" Momma whirled to look in Katherine's direction.

Katherine froze. She'd be discovered if she dared run so she stayed completely still and prayed whatever moved behind her would leave her be.

Silence fell. Even the birds went quiet and the squirrels scurried away. Dark clouds covered the sun, bringing dimness over the circle.

Momma must have been satisfied, because she focused again on the sun.

The breeze whistled against Katherine's ears as she inched around to scan the trees. Nothing. Cricket was nowhere in sight.

Momma now stood in the middle of the circle. A translucent figure materialized in front of her.

Katherine rubbed her eyes, but the misty silhouette remained. He shimmered in a spike of sunlight that beamed through the clouds. He was beautiful. Majestic. And Momma wasn't afraid.

Katherine recognized him immediately. It was the shaman from the road, this time with an elaborate headdress of long eagle feathers woven through leather fringe. Katherine nearly cried out when Momma took the hand he offered for fear he would transport her to another dimension.

What was going on? Momma stepped forward and fell into his embrace. They held tight to one another, the stones around the circle now aglow with their combined energy. Momma was crying.

Katherine had never seen Momma so vulnerable and peaceful. Did she need help? Was she bewitched?

When Katherine started to move from her hiding place, a strong arm pulled her back behind the tree.

"Don't, Katherine. Don't go in there." The singsong of his voice soothed her instantly. "This here is your momma's business. If she wants to hug a glowing medicine man, you can't do a thing about it."

"You can see him?" She turned into John's arms.

"Hush, girl, they'll hear us. She's leaving." He pressed his body intimately into hers to conceal them as Momma rode by atop Firefly. She shivered when she felt him so close.

"What's she doing? What's going on? Is Momma some kind of witch or-or alien or something?" Katherine whispered, trying to keep herself together.

She tucked her face into the curve of his neck and took in the enticing smell of his skin. For a moment, she forgot about the surreal scene she'd witnessed and concentrated instead on the warmth and firmness of his body against hers.

"Yes, Katherine. I saw 'im. She's no alien." He watched as Momma rode Firefly down the hill at a full gallop.

"Oh, thank God." She reluctantly pulled her head back up. "I was beginning to think I was nuts. That's the same man I saw the night of the accident. He's different than the old guy who appeared in my room the other night. I don't understand what's going on." She blew out a breath and nestled against his shoulder as if it was the most natural thing to do.

He put his arms around her and held her for a long moment, then finally asked, "You've been getting visits?"

She was thankful he didn't pull away when he asked the question. "Yes, I saw this one the same night I met you at the Sawgrass dance. He was standing in the middle of the road. You remember, the night Casey dumped the truck in the ditch?"

Sadness crept over her. She missed her friend more now than ever. "Casey left me on this blasted ranch after that happened."

John ignored her mention of Casey. "You said there was another one? In your room?"

The heat from his body penetrated her thin, cotton shirt. "Yes," she whispered into his ear. "He told me to *beware* of something. I have no idea what that means. Do you think he's talking about you?"

His voice was low and thoughtful. "Maybe they do mean me. My guess is they've been around you all your life and they're just now showing themselves. Maybe they mean to run me off." The sultry singsong of his voice clouded the message. She was focused on the closeness.

"Seems Momma has all the answers, if only she'd talk to me." She wrapped her arms around his waist and pulled him closer.

"Katherine, are you all right? What do you think you're doing?"

His eyes pulled at Katherine's heart when he backed away to look at her. Brazen need raced through her veins. "Would you kiss me, John Lattrell?"

He searched her eyes, unsure he'd heard her correctly. "What did you say?"

She gave him her best seductive smile and asked again. "I'd like you to kiss me."

"Nothing would please me more, Ms. Adams, but you're my boss's daughter. I'm pretty damn sure that's number one on the *what not to do at your new job* list."

Her look of disappointment must've done the trick. "Well, maybe one kiss won't hurt."

She took a surprised breath when he pulled her firmly into him.

He ran a finger along her jaw then tilted her chin up so their faces were an inch apart. Warm, sweet breath touched her lips. The strong arm he wrapped around her waist reminded her of the strap he tightened before his ride on Buckshot. Enticing. Confident. Irresistible. In control.

The sun sparkled in his ornery eyes as he searched hers once again to be sure. When he leaned in to place a tender kiss on her forehead, his lips felt soft and sure.

"Like this?" he whispered sensually, "Or like this?" He kissed her on the tip of her nose.

"Ah, ha." She sighed, licking her lips in anticipation. Her eyes closed as her need intensified. "Just like that."

"What about this?" He kissed each of her eyelids, then down over her cheekbones and along her jawline.

Katherine moaned when he moved the long, auburn strands of hair to the side to pinch his warm lips along the nape of her neck. When his mouth covered her tender earlobe, her knees buckled.

So, this was what love's all about. She'd never felt anything like this in her life. She hungered for more. "What are you doing to me?" She pushed the hat from his head and fisted his hair into her hands, pulling his mouth hard to hers. The soft whiskers of his goatee tickled just as she'd anticipated.

She took one lip between hers and then the other, exploring. When he touched his tongue to hers, the ache that started at the base of her stomach spread to every part of her body.

Moans of protest escaped when he tried to pull away. "Please don't stop." She wanted this feeling to last. She wanted him.

"But, Katherine." He fit his words between kisses. "This ain't right. It ain't . . ." When she pushed her hips into his, his voice went quiet as he held his breath.

Groans escaped when she felt him ready against her stomach. Desire with a tiny bit of fear drove her. "Oh, it's right, John. It's *so* right."

She melted on to the clover and pulled him down, intent on having him no matter what the consequences. Her long hair lay loose and wild against the ground. Heat rose on her skin.

John stared at her. She felt a twinge of pride at his apparent helplessness to deny her what she wanted. She wanted him and somehow, she knew what to do to accomplish her goal.

"Please, John." She brought her lips back to his and feasted. The front of his shirt was easy to unbutton. She was proud she hadn't fumbled. His breath caught as she trailed her fingernails through his chest hair and along the soft ribbon of fur leading down to his belt buckle.

She wasn't sure what she was doing, but she was figuring things out quickly. From his reaction, she was doing fine.

"Whoa, whoa, whoa." He caught her hand before it explored further.

"Please?" she whispered again.

He moved back from her to take a breath. His bicep pressed hard against the cotton sleeve as he ran his fingers through his hair, flustered. "We shouldn't be doing this, Katherine. This ain't right. You don't even know me. What if I'm a bad guy?" He leaned up on one elbow to look at her. "God, but you are beautiful. I must be crazy."

"Don't you want me?" Tears threatened as embarrassment overcame her. She sat up and straightened herself. "I'm sorry, I thought you—" She scrambled to her feet and walked away.

He followed, buttoning his shirt. "Sweet girl, don't you dare be sorry. I want you plenty. I'm already kicking myself right now." He placed his hat back on his head and reached for her, but she moved away.

"I'm pretty sure I'll never be loved, so you don't need to apologize." She looked down.

"Oh, you'll be loved, Katherine. There's no doubt. You're a fireball, you are." His words faded as he glanced toward the circle behind her. "What the hell?"

The shaman reappeared in solid form. And his eyes were trained on her.

"Beware, child." The words slipped into her mind. She looked back to John to see if he'd heard the warning, but all she saw was concern crinkle around his big blue eyes.

Caught between them, unsure what to do, she looked to John for answers.

"Katherine, no." He held out a hand.

"He's trying to tell me something. He's been trying to warn me, I know it. I need to find out what's going on."

Katherine backed away toward the circle. She had no fear. The shaman emanated safety and calm. He was gentle with Momma. Why would he harm her?

"What do you think you're gonna learn, Katherine?" John followed her until they stood just outside the circle. "Please, don't go in there."

She took one defiant step backward into the circle. "I'm gonna find out what he wants. I'm tired of this." She spun around and walked to the center.

At first, she felt nothing out of the ordinary. Instinctively, she followed the shaman as he spiraled in a circle with widespread arms. He chanted rhythmically to the eerie song made by the rain maker stick he shook.

Katherine forgot John stood at the edge of the circle. She forgot everything. She closed her eyes and let the energy flow through her. Suddenly smells of damp dirt and rain, jasmine and oak, permeated her senses, clearing away every remnant of fear and sadness.

Birds chirped loud, cheerful songs. All life around her became more vivid and alive. She felt rejuvenated.

She heard John's faint cries. "Come out of there, Katherine. You don't know what you're doing." But she didn't care. She only wanted to dance.

The shaman led her around the clockwise maze. She

chanted along with him. The power of the earth and the sky penetrated her soul.

"Katherine," John yelled again, loud enough to bring her attention away from the dance. When she looked back to the shaman, he was gone and the spell was broken. A single feather laid on the ground at her feet.

She spun one more time, her arms extended out to accept the powerful energy she felt inside the circle and then she walked to where John stood speechless, mesmerized by what he'd witnessed.

"I'll tell you this, John Lattrell. I've seen that this world holds a whole new energy for me. You're either with me on this journey or you're not."

She hesitated for a moment, giving him a chance to respond. When he said nothing, she pushed past him, more floating now than walking.

Katherine whistled for Cricket.

"Oh, no you don't." John trotted to catch her. "You can't walk away after what I just witnessed."

"I need to go. Momma'll be looking for me."

"You're still worried about what your Momma thinks after what you saw her do?"

She smiled and kicked at the dirt. "This here, and what we saw earlier, is our little secret. She can't ever know we saw her."

He raised a brow. "How could you not talk to her about this?"

She chuckled. "You're new here, so I'll give you this one, but trust me, if you plan to stick around Ruby's Ranch, you better never ever press my Momma on things she don't want to talk about. You were right earlier. This here's her business and what happened to me . . . is mine. Someday she and I will come to terms on this little secret."

He reached for her hand. "Okay, okay. I'll keep your

secret but what about you? What about that little ghost dance you performed?"

"I honestly have no idea what it all means. I know they mean me no harm. I feel more alive now than ever. I'll have to figure it out as I go."

John pulled his hat off and ran his fingers through his hair. "Well, okay, if you say so, but a second ago you were all over me. Now, after—whatever that was—you're ready to walk away."

Her eyes grabbed his with a new confidence. "Make no mistake, John Lattrell, I still want you. It's like a raging inside me. And I'll have you yet. Just not right now." She flung her long hair over her straightened shoulders and winked at him.

His face colored, which made him all the more endearing.

She swung her slender leg over the saddle and grabbed the reins.

"I'll see you at dinner. Don't you dare be late or Momma'll feed you to the coyotes."

And then she was gone. Cricket carried her away at a full run. Katherine felt so steady in the saddle it was like she wasn't sitting at all.

Chapter 16

Katherine made it out of the shower and into her apron five full minutes before Momma rode in from the far pasture. For once, she'd gotten away with something. At least for now.

She checked the meatloaf in the antique Wedgewood oven and stirred the potatoes boiling in the large canning pot. Green beans were washed, snapped, and set to steam with pieces of maple-cured bacon laid across the top to add flavor. Two large pans of cornbread sat ready for their turn in the oven, and vine-ripened tomatoes, sliced and paired with a handful of tender green onions, were displayed on her grandmother's large turkey platter.

Katherine's hands did the cooking while her mind wandered back to the hills behind the ranch, the mystical circle of rocks and Momma in the embrace of the glowing figure. The dance she shared with the shaman and John, so sexy, and strong even as he denied her what she wanted. The way he looked at her with those hungry, curious eyes. She ached to have him. She'd never get enough of that feeling.

Katherine admonished herself for the wicked thoughts and even more for the wicked smile. She had to be careful. Stan would catch on in an instant.

"I need a shower, I'm filthy. I'll be right in to help." Momma called as she slipped quickly through the kitchen door and hustled down the hall. "Smells wonderful, darling. Thanks for your help getting dinner going. Had a tangled calf up Haley's Peak. Took forever to get 'im loose."

"Sure, Momma. That was some calf, all right," Katherine mumbled under her breath. How long had Momma been visiting the circle and why did she keep it secret? Who or what was that celestial image? Did Stan know anything about it?

The potatoes smashed easily against the side of the pot when she checked if they were done. "It's no problem, Momma. Potatoes are ready to mash and I'm putting the cornbread in now," she yelled down the hall as Momma closed the bathroom door.

The perfectly browned meat bubbled around the edges when Katherine pulled it from the oven. She guided the pans of bread in carefully, avoiding burning her hand on the hot, metal sides. She spooned grease from the loaf pans into a large skillet to make gravy.

As Katherine stirred milk into the fried grease and flour, she daydreamed about how it felt to be touched by John, and how much she'd hated it when he'd pulled away. How it felt to be enveloped by the love and acceptance of the shaman.

Out of the corner of her eye she caught the reflection of the old man in the shiny chrome backsplash. His head looked disproportionately large compared to his body. He stared at her with blank, expressionless eyes.

"Oh, my God." She jerked away from the skillet, splashing hot gravy over the top of her hand and all over the floor. When she looked up, he was gone, but his voice clanged loud in her mind.

"Beware, child." A whisper on the unmoving air.

Her eyes darted around the kitchen expecting him to appear somewhere else. But he and his voice were gone.

"What do you want from me?" she asked. Worry replaced her sensual daydreams of John.

Her hand burned like she'd been stung by a hornet.

"Ow, ow, ow." She tossed the wooden spoon into the sink and ran cold water over her wound.

"Tell me why I should beware?" she yelled in frustration.

"Katherine?" Momma questioned when she walked into the kitchen and spied the raised red blister and the mess of gravy on the floor. "Jesus, girl. What happened?" She took Katherine's hand to survey the damage.

Momma patted Katherine's hand dry with a clean dishcloth then spread a layer of cool, softened butter across the angry burn which instantly calmed the sting. The roll of gauze from the kitchen drawer was long enough to wrap loosely around the wound to protect from infection. Momma tucked the end of the gauze under the edge to keep it secure.

"Keep it dry. We'll check it after dinner to be sure you don't need Doc to have a look at it." She let go of Katherine's hand, but held her eyes for a second longer. "You okay, kiddo?"

Katherine wanted so much to ask about the shaman, but she'd only close down again. "I'm fine, Momma. Just slipped out of my hand."

"Okay then." She squinted at Katherine, like she was making sure of something, then turned to finish dinner.

Once the mess on the floor was cleaned up, Momma salvaged the remaining gravy from the pan and dumped the potatoes in a large metal colander to drain in the sink.

"See if you can manage these." Momma dumped the potatoes back into the empty pot and placed the large potato masher in Katherine's good hand.

The kitchen buzzed with life as the two of them worked silently on the country feast. The smells of the cornbread browning in the oven mixed with fresh onions and homemade meatloaf had Katherine's stomach growling.

Momma was a whirl with the final dinner preparations. She dipped the green beans into a large blue willow serving bowl, then sliced the meatloaf in perfect portions on to a matching platter. She pulled the cornbread from the oven at the peak of crispiness and smeared it with melted butter. She dissolved sugar into the warm-from-the-sun brewed tea and poured it into the ice filled mason jars she'd set out on the counter.

Katherine helped as much as she could without undoing the bandage. She kept her eyes trained on the path from the corrals. John would be walking into her door at any moment, and she could hardly contain herself.

How would she keep her cool when he sat at Momma's table and captured her with those deep blue eyes? If she didn't monitor her reaction, it would be over before it ever started.

"Katherine." Momma handed her the plate of cut cornbread to carry to the table. "Is somethin' bothering you? I thought I heard you talking to yourself earlier?"

The plate bobbled so much in Katherine's hands, a piece of hot buttered bread hit the wood floor with a splat.

Momma reached for the platter just in time to salvage the rest. "Girl, you're a mess today. What's wrong with you?"

Katherine knew she'd have to explain when she saw the concerned look in Momma's eyes. Otherwise, she wouldn't give her a moment's peace.

"I-I've been seeing things." She bent down to pick up the piece of bread to toss it into the trash can.

Momma placed the platter of cornbread on the counter and took her daughter by the shoulders. She explored her frightened eyes. "What do you mean, *seeing* things?"

When Katherine tried to look away, Momma caught her chin and forced her gaze back up. "What is it? Tell me this instant."

Katherine fought tears. She feared Momma's reaction more than her visiting ghosts.

"I told you about the shaman in the road the night of the accident. You remember?" Katherine saw tension form on Momma's face. Her cheeks went white and her eyes widened.

"It's true, Momma. And then the other night an old man appeared in my room. He looked like a cloud. He told me to beware, but I don't understand what he's warning me about. What does he mean, Momma?"

"Katherine Ann, what kind of craziness are you talking?" Momma tried to pull back, but Katherine stopped her.

"Momma, I know you believe me. Why won't you talk to me about this?" Tears of frustration rolled down her face.

"Enough!"

"Please, Momma, you know I'm telling the truth," she asked, her heart crushed. She felt alone. Betrayed.

Momma backed away and avoided Katherine's gaze. She gave no sympathy or understanding. The denial made Katherine shrink inside. The first time she'd confided in her about something important and this was her reaction? No support. Not even concern.

"Why won't you talk to me?" Katherine's voice trailed away as Momma picked up the cornbread and headed into the dining room.

"We're done talking about this, Katherine. You hear me? Done!"

"I saw you, you know," Katherine whispered, after Momma left the room. She didn't turn back.

Stan stood in the kitchen doorway, his eyes sad and regretful.

"Come here, darlin. I'm so sorry." He took Katherine in his arms and held tight. "You know your Momma. She shuts down if you push 'er." He brushed the hair away from her red, swollen eyes. "It's all right, honey. She'll come around."

Katherine looked at him in dismay. "Stan, I'm telling the truth and she knows it. What's wrong with her? Does she hate me? Are these people trying to harm me?"

"Oh, honey, you know she loves you. She thinks she's helping you. Your Momma doesn't understand it herself. God knows she's been trying for years."

Katherine backed away from him, startled, upset to think her only ally kept such an important secret from her. "What do you mean, *she doesn't understand it*? What's going on?"

The look he gave told her everything she needed to know. Ghosts or visions followed the whole family and Momma hadn't warned her about it? Why wouldn't Momma talk to her about it? What did the spirits want?

Stan shook his head, unable to find the words to answer her questions. "I'm sorry, honey. I don't know what to tell you."

He fidgeted. He felt helpless too, she knew it, because he loved Momma. No one ever said it out loud, but it was sweet and obvious all the same. He protected her no matter what. He stood by her side come hell or high water. All he could do was be there when things stopped making sense. Which they often did.

"Well, I'll be damned if I let this ruin my life like it's ruined Momma's. How long has this been going on? What do they want?" She rattled off questions, one after the other, to a man who had no answers.

Or did he know more than he was willing to tell?

Chapter 17

The boys filed in, one at a time, boots on the porch and hats on the rack. Each knew better than to come to Momma's table without a proper bath, a clean shave, and fresh clothes. If they arrived after the blessing, they knew not to even bother.

The men of Ruby's Ranch were a scraggly bunch on the range, but a right handsome group of gents at Momma's table. Dutch and JB, strongly built and faithful to one another and to Momma, sat side by side. Young Kelly always near Stan. Casey's chair, now empty, would be John's place from now on. The Adams women sat prominently at each end of the table as a symbolic and real show of authority.

When John walked through the front door, his familiar smile caught Katherine unprepared. Stan faded from view when she sank into the safety of John's eyes, her need to be in his arms more desperate now.

Stan placed a hand on her shoulder in warning. "Watch yourself with him, Kat. Your Momma can't take you falling for him the same day she discovered you've inherited the family curse. It's too much. She's more fragile than you know."

"Momma, fragile? Please, Stan, spare me." Katherine pushed his hand away, uninterested in hearing about Momma's vulnerability. She wanted to tell him what she'd witnessed in the circle, but she didn't dare. He wouldn't help her if she did. She knew that now.

As the boys found their seats around the table, Katherine trained her stare on John. Unashamed. Brazen.

She stretched her good hand across the table and greeted him. "Hello, John. So nice to see you again."

When she clutched his hand and batted her eyelashes, Momma and every other person around the table saw something more was brewing between them than a casual hello.

"Pleasure to see you again, Miss Adams." He tried to let go of her hand when he recognized the slack-jawed warning from the boys around the table. A few even shook their heads.

Katherine smiled the kind of smile that gave away more than she'd want to in a saner moment. "A pleasure, indeed."

She giggled, then let his hand slip from hers when Dutch ribbed John in the side. The energy between them dimmed when their hands disconnected.

Momma placed the last plate of meatloaf at the far end of the table and slowly walked to where her daughter stood, still blatantly ogling John.

Katherine shied away when Momma reached for her. Her disapproving look was set to destroy John's interest in her baby girl.

"Young man, seems as though we need to get a few things straight right now. Katherine here is my *only* daughter. She's only sixteen!"

"Momma!" Katherine gasped. "I'm—"

But Momma barreled ahead as if Katherine hadn't spoken. "She apologizes for being so forward and I apologize for not teaching her to behave more appropriately in mixed company." Momma's hands were on her hips, threatening.

John's expression changed from playful to panic as the words sunk in. Katherine could almost see him mouth "Sixteen." He turned away and shook his head, shocked at the mess he'd inadvertently stepped into.

"John, she's lying. I'm eighteen. I swear it!"

Katherine's heart deflated when he let out a sigh of

disbelief. He ducked his head and took a seat demurely at her Momma's table.

Her knight in shining armor hadn't defended her. He hadn't said, I don't care how old she is—I love her. John Lattrell was her last hope and he'd failed. Humiliation colored her cheeks.

Why couldn't at least one person stand up to Momma? What was this power she held?

"Now you." Momma pointed to Katherine. "You take your flirty little self to your room and stay there until you learn some manners." She spun Katherine away from the uncomfortable crowd of men and nudged her out of the dining room. "Go, young lady. That's the end of it."

Katherine looked over her shoulder to John again who stared in silence at his folded hands. Stan shook his head, obviously unsure how to help.

"Yes, Momma." She ran down the long, rose-colored hallway, away from the awkward confrontation. Tears streamed down her cheeks.

The last thing she heard before slamming her bedroom door, was Momma demanding the boys start eating while the food was still hot, apologizing for her daughter's behavior.

Katherine's stomach churned as anger and humiliation mixed with hurt. Momma would even lie to get her way. And seeing John pull away was devastating. Even Augie's loving support couldn't soothe her. Tears flowed as she quietly pulled out her packed bag from the back of the closet, gathered her money and paints, and slipped out her bedroom window. She ran as fast as her booted feet could carry her across the front field and onto the road.

This was the last time she'd ever be embarrassed by Momma. She had to escape this certain hell or she'd surely die.

Chapter 18

Katherine's grand adventure started in the back of an old Ford pickup, wedged between cages of laying hens making their way to a new home away from the Kern River Valley. An old German shepherd named Rufus laid his tired head comfortably in her lap as they rumbled down the bumpy country road. She had no idea where her journey was taking her, but she was already calmer getting away from Ruby's Ranch. She was bound and determined to find her own way.

She played the confrontation over and over in her mind, each time tears freshened and her heart ached. If Momma loved her as much as she professed, how could she treat her so cruelly, especially in front of other people? Other people like John Lattrell who caved so easily from the pressure.

She scooted down and laid her head against the warm shepherd. He smelled of fresh grass. "Thank you, boy." She rubbed his leg when he nuzzled in to sniff her hair then licked a broad, wet kiss across her cheek.

Katherine didn't know when she fell asleep, or for how long she'd slept, but dawn had broken when the truck pulled to a halt in front of the General Store in a town she didn't recognize.

The old couple crawled slowly out of the cab of the truck and greeted the shepherd and their weary passenger.

"Good boy, you kept our new friend company I see." The gentle man smiled a broad, crooked smile when he spoke. "Sorry if he bothered you, honey."

"Oh no, sir. He's the sweetest thing. He kept me warm."

Katherine sat up and straightened her clothes, wincing with pain from the wound on her hand.

"Hungry, honey?" The old woman asked. "Come on now, jump down from there and we'll get you a bite to eat before you continue on your journey." There was a kindness and understanding about her Katherine had never seen before.

She hopped from the tail gate and strapped her bag against her back. "I couldn't impose, ma'am. I do appreciate the ride." Her eyes dropped.

"Not an imposition, little lady." The gentleman shuffled around the rear of the truck and nudged her forward toward Nell's Country Diner at the corner of the block.

The woman looked her over, seeing something desperate there, Katherine was sure. Then she smiled a non-judgmental smile.

"I don't know what you're running from, little lady, but you won't get far with no food in your belly." She grabbed Katherine's hand and led her into the diner.

Katherine had never seen so many roosters in her entire life. Salt and pepper shakers, pictures, huge ceramic statues, even the wall paper depicted thousands of chickens milling around in a barnyard scene. A handful of hard-working patrons slumped over steaming cups of black coffee, chattered away to one another about the weather and such things, paying them no mind. Katherine was thankful no one looked familiar.

As she followed the woman to the table, Katherine noticed the fine stitching on her well-worn, freshly pressed smock. Hand-knitted socks peeked out from the tops of her dirty boots. She smelled of liniment and lavender. When she sat her wide bottom against the vinyl seat, a poof of air escaped the cushion, which made her chuckle, playfully.

"That was the seat, I promise."

Katherine couldn't help but smile.

The diner smelled like Momma's kitchen on a Sunday morning. There was sausage, pork chops, and bacon frying loudly on the grill—fresh biscuits baking in the oven. Katherine's stomach growled so loud she was sure everyone within ten feet could hear.

"Sam," the old woman called to the tall, gangly young man behind the counter. "We'll have three of your breakfast specials, bacon and hash browns crispy, orange juice and black coffee all around." She looked curiously at Katherine who sat quietly at the other side of the booth, sniffing at the divine aroma coming from the little kitchen in the back.

"You drink coffee, honey?" The scarf she wore around her short, gray hair, fell against her shoulders when she tugged the tie. Silver and turquoise horseshoe earrings hung from her long lobes. Her pale green eyes sparkled in delight when she saw Katherine's careful curiosity.

"Coffee, honey?" she asked again, reaching across the table to pat Katherine's fidgeting hand.

"That'd be very nice, ma'am. Thank you." Katherine finally answered, appreciating the warmth and concern emanating from her touch.

"Now let me see what you've done to your hand," she said, gently holding Katherine's hand to unravel the gauze. "May I?"

Katherine nodded, her eyes wide.

"Mmmmm-hmmm. Looks a might irritated." The quarter-sized blister had flattened in her journey, but the skin was still bright red and inflamed.

The old woman opened her bag and pulled out a bottle of witch hazel and a fresh cotton ball to clean the wound. She then smoothed on some aloe gel from a tube and dotted a drop of lavender oil in the middle and worked it in. Instantly, the burn calmed.

"Here honey, you take these and do this twice a day until that burn's all healed." She bundled the items together and slipped them into a small silk pouch and handed them to Katherine. "Let's put a nice wrap to keep it clean," she added as she placed a clean bandage over the area and wrapped it with tape from her bag.

"Thank you so much, ma'am. You're too kind," Katherine said, accepting the remaining gauze and tape.

"No trouble at all, sweetie. I make these liniments myself. Mostly 'cause that husband of mine is constantly gettin' banged up." She winked and smiled.

The old man made his way from the restroom and scooted in next to the old woman. "You order, darlin?"

"Yes, indeed. The usual."

Sam smiled curiously at Katherine as he served the coffees and orange juice. When he laid the napkin rolled utensils in front of her he nodded a greeting. "Welcome to Nell's Diner, Miss."

"Sam, this here's a friend of ours." The old man paused and looked across at Katherine, perplexed he couldn't come up with her name.

"I'm Kat." She took his damp hand into hers. "I'm just passing through. Can you tell me where I can find the bus station?" She smiled with fake confidence.

"Good to know you, Miss Kat. The bus station is up a few blocks, behind the hardware store there on 3rd and Elm. You can't miss it. Not sure when the bus runs today. All depends on where you're headed, I suspect?"

All three of them looked to her for a response. She picked up the glass of juice and drank, stalling to come up with an answer. She had no idea where she was going, only that she was heading as far from the Kern River Valley as she could manage.

Thankfully, the cook banged the counter bell with his metal spatula, alerting Sam to pick up an order. Katherine took another drink as he walked away. Relieved.

The old woman reached across the table to pat her hand again. "You keep your plans to yourself, sweetie. It ain't no one's business."

Katherine thanked the woman with a nod and a loud exhale.

"Here we go, three specials, extra crispy." Sam set the large plates of food in front of each of them and backed away, looking at Katherine, hoping still for an answer. She dismissed him with a thank you, looking down at the plate. She hoped he'd take the hint and walk away.

The plate of food looked like a picture straight out of a country cooking magazine. If it tasted half as good as it looked, she was in for a treat. The bacon was perfectly charred at the edges. The butter-fried eggs perched against a large flat of golden, crispy hash browns. The huge flaky biscuit, covered in homemade sausage gravy, smelled divine.

Katherine hadn't realized how hungry she was until the food was laid out in front of her. No dinner last night coupled with the stress of running away made her ravenous.

"Oh, this looks amazing, thank you," she said to the couple who'd already dug in.

"Eat up, honey. You're skin and bones." The old man smiled with a piece of bacon sticking out of his mouth.

Katherine didn't take another breath until she finished sopping the last bit of gravy from the plate with the last bite of biscuit.

The old couple, she found out, were Jed and Mable Baxter, from Willow Cove, a little hamlet way up in the mountains above Sierra Mount. They raised chickens to sell at the farmer's markets, trading sometimes for other animals or fresh fruit and vegetables to can. They were angels dropped from heaven as far as Katherine was concerned.

She was thankful they didn't ask questions. Maybe they sensed she wasn't interested in answering.

After breakfast, they walked her to the bus station to be sure she was really okay to travel on by herself. Before she stepped through the ticket door she turned to look at them. "Thank you both, so much." She hugged them. "I appreciate your kindness and generosity more than you'll ever know."

Jed bent in for a half-hug and patted her gently on the shoulder. "You be safe on your adventure, darling." He looked her in the eye, then backed away and spoke toward his wife. "Mable, honey, I'll be in the store there when you're done." He shuffled toward Kinney's Hardware store, dragging one well-worn boot slightly behind.

Mable stood silently, watching her, calculating. "Listen, honey. I don't want to know where you're headed, 'cause I don't want to have to lie when someone comes looking for you. I want you to find whatever it is you're searching for out there, but you need to *beware*, child. There's people out there who'd take advantage of a pretty little country girl like you. Real bad people."

The old woman reached into her large cloth handbag again and pulled out a small roll of bills, and a leather pouch with a dreamcatcher stitched on the front.

"You take this here to help you find your way." Mable held out the gifts for Katherine to take.

"Oh, no, ma'am, I can't accept this. It wouldn't be right. You've already given me so much." Katherine held up a hand to deflect. "I appreciate it, but I can do this on my own. Really. You've done enough already." She tried to sound convincing.

Mable continued to hold the items in front of her, intent on Katherine accepting them. "Miss Kat, you have quite a journey ahead of you. You need to accept this kindness to make it to your destiny. You need to accept it so I can also find my own way." A tear of sincerity formed at the corner of her weary eyes. "Take it, for me. Please."

Katherine knew she had to accept the gift. Not sure why, but it was true all the same. Katherine stepped forward and took the gifts and stuffed them into her pack, then she took the frail woman into her arms once again.

"I'll never forget you, Miss Mable. Not ever. I can't thank you enough."

When she pulled away from the old woman she blinked against her sanity. Mable had turned into the old man who'd come to her in her dreams, his sharp features replaced Mable's sweet, weathered face.

Katherine didn't flinch away from him this time. Instead she pulled him back into her arms. The leather smock felt smooth against her cheek. "Thank you," she whispered.

"Go now," he said to her. "You have your destiny to follow." And then he turned back into the kindly old woman. A knowing smile crossed her thin lips.

Chapter 19

The bus was empty aside from a young mother cradling her sleeping baby and a blind man, tapping the foot bar in front of him with his cane. When they pulled out of the station, there was no sign of the old couple or the truck that had carried her to this place. Only a stray dog eating scraps thrown in the alley behind the diner, and Sam waving as they slowly drove by.

She reached into her bag and pulled out the gifts the old woman had given her. She counted two hundred in twenty-dollar bills. A single owl feather was tucked in the small leather pouch. She placed the other three feathers she'd gathered into the pouch and put it safely back into her bag before laying down in the seat to take a much-needed nap.

Katherine rode the bus as far south as the line would take her, which landed her squarely in the middle of a loud, chaotic city with more people on one street corner than she imagined lived in her entire home town. Beyond the tall buildings, she spotted the ocean with tiny sailboats gliding slowly across the brilliant aqua horizon.

By now Momma would have discovered her missing from her room and set plans in motion to hunt her down and drag her back to the ranch. Katherine knew they'd easily track her this far, so she had little time to scatter from the station, leaving no scents to follow.

The station buzzed with the movement and chatter of dozens of passengers waiting to board various buses to destinations unknown. Jim Morrison rang out loud over the speakers. Young girls with dark suntans and sun-bleached hair displayed their bodies in ways Katherine never imagined. Halter tops and short shorts worn with tall wedge sandals and long, dangling jewelry. Many wore colorful tie-dye hippy skirts and matching headbands. Their eyes were bright red from smoking only God knew what.

Katherine slowly climbed down from the bus and took in the sea of interesting, curious faces. She felt eyes on her from all around. This time not in envy or awe, most likely wondering where on earth she'd come from wearing her country getup.

"Yee-haw," yelled a particularly scruffy blonde, laughing with her friends. The thick, black eyeliner circling her sharp gold eyes made her appear more cat than human. "Where's your horse, little cowgirl?"

Katherine felt the insult down to her bones. Instead of turning the other cheek as she'd been taught, she challenged the girl who wreaked of clove cigarettes and body odor. There was a seriousness in the girl's eyes that defied her age. It was obvious she'd led a hard life, probably without a single person who really cared. That still didn't give her the right to be rude.

When she snarled her hee-haw again, Katherine snapped back. "What's your problem?" She felt suddenly protective of her country heritage. "You intimidated by a fully clothed woman? I feel sorry for you, having to be half naked to get attention. You need to back off, 'cause this little country girl can drop you like a light if you're not careful. Now move!" Katherine was proud of how well she channeled Momma.

The girl was shocked, Katherine could tell. She backed away, then looked at her feet, embarrassed when the crowd laughed. She'd been put in her place by a boot-wearing cowgirl and she didn't like it. Katherine expected no one had ever stood up to her before.

Every eye followed Katherine as she tossed the bag over her shoulder and pushed past the girl. She needed to freshen up and change out of her country garb. The more people who saw her, the more chance she'd be caught before the day was out.

Why'd I do that? Calling attention to myself is a great idea! Idiot! She admonished herself for making a scene as she pushed opened the filthy restroom door.

The warm, dank space smelled like the sewer itself. An exhausted girl reflected back at her in the mirror. Her usually wavy hair was now flat on one side from sleeping on the bus. When she removed the bandage from her hand to splash water on her face, she was shocked to see the blister had all but disappeared. "Well, I'll be. That's amazing." She tossed the bandage into the overflowing trash can, then ran wet fingers through her hair to bring it back to life.

She closed herself into the stall and changed from her jeans and boots to her little blue dress and the only pair of flip-flops she'd ever owned.

She pulled her long hair into a messy ponytail at the back of her head. The peasant dress was unbuttoned all the way to show a little cleavage. She swiped extra makeup across her face, to try and blend in with the brightly colored teen crowd she'd witnessed. A cheap pair of mirrored sunglasses, and a Hostess Twinkie from the station store, and she was just another beach bum, a hippy in the crowd.

In spite of being near the ocean, the streets around the bus station smelled of urine and smoke. Horns honked so loud Katherine couldn't hear herself think. She didn't know how to function in the chaos. A delivery van nearly ran her down when she crossed against the light.

She got turned around trying to work her way to the beach. There were no recognizable landmarks or trees to help guide her way. People chattered around her like the chirp of a million birds, many in unrecognizable languages. She felt invisible and alone in a sea of faces, almost paralyzed by all the foreign sights and smells.

She had to get a grip, quit whining. This was what she wanted. City, culture, excitement, and interesting, new people everywhere. What was her problem?

"You lost, Miss?" A middle-aged man stood next to her at the crosswalk, squinting against the bright sun at her back. She couldn't believe he even noticed her in the confusion of cars and bodies. When she got a good look at him, she wished he hadn't.

His dark hair was slicked back with a strong-smelling oil, his black mustache so bushy it covered his teeth. The mismatched clothes he wore looked to be a size too small, his arms hairier than any she'd ever seen. His pungent breath smelled of garlic and some other foreign spices they'd never used in Momma's kitchen.

"Can you point me toward the ocean, please," she asked, smiling innocently. She tried her best to keep her distance as he ran his tongue through the overgrown mustache.

"I'm happy to walk with you, if you'd like." His devilish smile reminded her of a red-tailed hawk hovering over prey. Her internal alarm rang loud inside her head as his hungry eyes blatantly grazed her body. "Wouldn't you like that?"

Katherine tried to move away from the unyielding crowd of people. Panic and disgust crawled up her spine when his sweating body touched hers.

"I don't think so, sir. I'll find it on my own." She pushed her way through the shoulder-to-shoulder throng of people walking along the sidewalk, sidestepping the homeless who laid on their makeshift beds along the buildings.

Sadness and fear crept over her when she saw how these people lived. Maybe they too had yearned for the excitement of the city, and found themselves alone and destitute, now living on the streets.

"Katherine!"

She whirled around and searched the crowd. No one

here knew her name. Surely they hadn't already found her. A sea of faces greeted her, all unconcerned.

She turned, tucked her bag tight under her arm, and ran.

The screech of brakes and the smell of exhaust felt like wolves at her heels. She had to get ahead of the stench to discover the beauty and culture she'd always dreamed of. It had to be here somewhere.

What she wouldn't give to whistle for Cricket to get away. She moved as quickly as she could along the uneven sidewalks, dodging street vendors, and rolled-up carpets being peddled by loud salesmen shouting at passersby.

A sharp pain stitched under her ribs, forcing her to stop and catch a breath. When she looked down, she realized she'd lost one of her flip-flops during her escape.

"Seriously?" she said to the pigeons that swarmed around searching for a morsel of food.

When she leaned against a wide brick window sill to pull on her boots, she looked up to see a line of funky art galleries across the street. Brilliant watercolors of beach scenes and children displayed the exceptional talent of the local artists. No longer trapped by a crowd of angry people bustling about. Rather, smartly-dressed socialites were seated under sidewalk umbrellas, drinking lemon-wedged waters around potted flowering trees. Even the stench in the air had changed to the scent of sweet lavender blossoms riding on the chilled mist of the ocean.

Katherine straightened herself and applied another layer of strawberry lip gloss before she crossed the street. She shook off the angst she'd felt for the city and shoved her shoulders back, added a sway to her walk. She wanted to fit in, but it was awkward.

She didn't know how to be anything but a rancher's daughter. She didn't mind her boots had manure under them, or her simple dress was the finest she owned, she wanted to live this life for a moment, like she was born in the city, amongst the stars.

A whistle followed her when she stopped to gawk into a window where a painting of ducklings swimming in a pond looked eerily like Momma's pond back at Ruby's Ranch. Why would people who lived in this amazing city want to buy a painting from a little country ranch?

A second whistle rang out, this time closer. She looked across the street toward the sound and blinked to clear her sight. "What the devil?" She whispered to herself in disbelief. "Casey?"

"Casey!" She yelled as she ran across the street, so happy to see a friendly face she didn't think how odd it was for him to be there.

Casey stood tall and tanned in his Bermuda shorts and Beach Bum T-shirt, his sun-bleached hair no longer captured by a cowboy hat and his feet no longer trapped inside hot leather boots. He had a sparkle now, a light he didn't have when he left Ruby's Ranch. It gave Katherine hope to see he hadn't withered and died leaving the ranch.

"Kat, are you all right?" He panted. "You sure are hard to catch." He held out her lost flip-flop.

Tears came to her eyes when she jumped into his arms and let him hold her. "It's so good to see you," she whispered. "So good."

He squeezed a little tighter, then set her back down. "You're a sight for sore eyes yourself, but Kat, what have you done, running off like that? Your momma is sick with worry."

She almost stumbled back. "What do you mean? How did you know?" She was dumbfounded and pulled her bag closer. Should she run again?

"Kat, wait." Casey held out a pleading hand. "Stan knew I was staying with my mom down here. Once they figured out you'd come south, he figured you might be headed to see me." He looked down now, sad. "I told him you definitely wouldn't be looking for me." His voice broke.

Katherine leaned in and laid a kiss on his cheek. "I'm sorry, Casey, I didn't know you were living down here."

"I told him that."

"How'd you find me?"

He shrugged. "I said I'd check out a few bus stations. Pure luck I got to this one as you came out it. By the time I parked, I almost lost you. Then you started running. I never knew you could run like that, whew."

"So, what are you supposed to do now, call 'em? Are they on their way here or are they already here?" Oppression washed over her as she felt the adventure coming to a premature end.

"Come on." Ignoring her questions, he grabbed her hand and led her across the street toward the beach. "Take off those boots, Kat. You need to feel the sand between your toes."

Chapter 20

They walked along the wet sand for a long while. Katherine watched the seagulls circle over the foamy waves and the nearly naked sun-worshippers frolic along the shore. All the sights she'd never seen in her life. She let her hair down so the cool ocean breeze could blow calmness over her body. Casey held her hand and talked with her as though nothing could ever break the spell.

"So, really," she finally said, keeping her eyes on the horizon. "How long do I have before they come?"

"They're not coming, Kat."

She frowned at him. She dropped the hand he held. "What do you mean, they're not coming?"

"Stan said to keep an eye on you if I found you."

"I don't understand."

Casey raked his long fingers through his hair and shook his head. "For such a smart girl, you really surprise me sometimes."

"Stop it! What's going on?"

"Stan called Doc out to give your momma something to calm her down. She's gone batty worried about you, so she needed to get some rest so she could be rational."

Katherine stopped and sat in the sand. "What does that mean?"

"I need to call him, Kat, so he's not worried, but he said if you showed up, it'd be okay for you to stay a bit. He's hoping you'll get this need to be off the ranch out of your system. He's gonna tell your Momma you're safe and give her a little time to gather herself. And give you time away." Casey sat beside her and threw a rock into the ocean.

"I don't wanna go back, Casey. I'll never get this need out of my system and we both know Momma'll never come around. Stan's dreaming." She leaned her head on Casey's shoulder and prayed. "I don't know what to do. Should I keep running?"

Casey stayed quiet and still for a good long time, letting her cuddle next to him.

She yawned and took in a few deep breaths. "Casey." Her voice was barely loud enough to hear. "I'm starving!"

He smiled and kissed the top of her head. "I can't fix all the crap with your momma, but I can definitely fix that. There's a mean burger joint on the pier. My treat."

Katherine nearly jumped to her feet. "A burger sounds amazing, let's go."

~ ~ ~

The next few days, Casey and Katherine explored. The city lights at night captured her heart, but the chaos was still a little overwhelming. The ocean and Casey's calmness soothed her as she learned more and more about life in the city. Drug use and night life—everything that made this part of California infamous in the 1960s—made her uneasy. She hadn't realized just how sheltered a life she'd been living.

Casey borrowed his mom's car and bought a map of movie stars' homes. He drove Katherine over the routes in Beverly Hills, then they strolled the Hollywood Walk of Fame. They walked along Rodeo Drive, taking in the glitz and glamour of expensive jewelry and clothing that most likely cost more than the entire summer's herd at Ruby's Ranch.

Katherine found it interesting they'd named a ritzy city street after a country event. This place was like no rodeo she'd ever seen.

"This is all so much to take in. I envy you getting to live here," Katherine said as they ate foot-long hotdogs from a street vendor.

"What do you mean, *envy me*? This is a terrible life. No one cares at all about anyone else. It's loud and smells like exhaust and street people. I hate it here. Except for the ocean. The water is the only reason I can stand it." He wolfed down the dog in five quick bites, and drank lemonade from a Styrofoam cup.

"This is horrible. Not like country lemonade where they squeeze actual lemons." He dumped the wrapper and the drink into the trash can and wiped his hands with the thin paper napkin.

Katherine looked at him curiously. "How could you hate it here? It's so full of life."

"Kat, I'm only here because my doctor hasn't released me to ride. I'm still having headaches. The minute I'm able, I'm leaving here and finding a new ranch. I miss it so much." His eyes caught hers, trying to make her understand ranching and country life was his serenity. "I missed you too."

She ducked from his warm gaze, wrapped the second half of her hotdog and offered it to him. "You want this? I can't eat it." She took a drink of her lemonade and had to agree. This was no country lemonade and since no one in the city seemed to even know what sweet tea was, she too dumped her drink into the trash along with the dog he'd declined.

"Can we go back to your mom's? I feel like I need to lay down." She rubbed her stomach, trying to smooth away the lump of hot dog that sat there, unmoved.

"Whatever you want, darlin'." He took her hand again, something she'd become accustomed to, and led her along the alleyway behind the big department stores, toward the lot where they'd parked his mother's Ford Pinto. Homeless people huddled around trash cans, searching for food. Katherine felt guilty she'd discarded her lunch instead of offering it to someone in need.

All the way to Casey's house, she looked down at her hands and away from the road, to keep from flinching in the stop and go traffic. Too many cars in such a small space made her nervous. And Casey saying he missed her and calling her darlin'. He knew they were still nothing but friends, right?

Nausea from the anxiety and the questionable lunch built. All she wanted was a nice comfortable bed and a few hours' sleep. What she wouldn't give for one of Momma's gingerbread cookies right about now.

Chapter 21

Casey's mother, Clara, could easily pass for his older sister. Her long, white blond hair was thick and curly like his, her eyes alive with unaffected compassion. She spent most of her time braless, in billowy jersey dresses and beaded necklaces which hung to her navel. She did some kind of work in Hollywood, but Katherine never quite understood what. Makeup or personal assistant, something where she rubbed elbows daily with the stars.

Each morning Clara laid out an array of fresh fruit and store-bought scones for them to eat, along with bitter coffee and raw milled sugar. She was vegetarian, which seemed odd to Katherine, since her son and her ex-husband were both in the cattle business.

The morning after their hot dog lunch, Katherine took a long, hot, fabulous shower using handmade goat milk soap and coconut oil for conditioner.

Feeling clean and refreshed, Katherine sat at the table and picked at a blueberry scone, choosing water over the strong coffee. The crystal wind chimes that hung from the chandelier jingled in the gentle breeze blowing through the open sliding glass door.

Casey sang a country ballad from the shower, which sharply contrasted the street band cranking out loud rock music from the park across the street.

Clara glided around the kitchen like a fairy princess without a care in the world. So different than Momma, who was thoughtful and methodical with every task.

"So, sweetheart, how far along are you?" The older woman smiled a brilliant, blushing smile as she refilled Katherine's water from a hand-painted pitcher.

Katherine eyes widened as she pushed back from the table. "Excuse me? Did you ask how far *along* I am?" She wasn't sure she'd heard her right. She prayed she hadn't.

"Why yes, look at you. You're all a-bloom. Flushing cheeks, glowing aura. You're definitely with child. Are you not?" She continued to smile at Katherine, even though her sentiments had hit her guest square in the chest.

Katherine shook her head. "Oh no, no, ma'am. That's not possible."

"What's not possible?" Casey asked, rounding the corner wearing a new pair of Bermudas with a golden sunset branded across the front. His stomach and chest were toned and tan. He immediately stopped rubbing the towel over his wet hair when he saw the panic rising in Katherine's eyes. "Kat, what is it? What's wrong?" He sat at the other end of the table.

Clara looked from her son to Katherine and back again. "Well, it seems as though your young friend didn't realize she's with child. I hope you're planning on doing right by her, young man." She poured a second glass of water and set it in front of Casey, then sat herself and nibbled at a scone.

"You're pregnant?" He looked at Katherine, frustration and hurt welling again. "Is that why you ran off, Kat?"

She shook her head. "There's no way I'm pregnant, Casey. No way. I couldn't be."

"Kat?" His eyes blurred with tears. "It's John's, isn't it? What the hell? That damn idiot!" Casey threw the towel to the floor and moved the water glass away to avoid knocking it off the table.

She reached for his hand, but he pulled away. "She's wrong, Casey. I promise you." She brought her hands to her face and let the tears flow, unable to stop them now. He didn't believe her.

"Oh dear, I'm sorry." Clara stood to leave them alone. She looked to her son, now no longer smiling. "Sometimes my sight is off, sweetheart. You know that. I'm very sorry, young lady." She retreated from the room quickly, sloshing her coffee over the sides of her cup.

"Jesus, Kat. Jesus." He stood to pace, doing his best not to yell. Anger and hurt vibrated from him.

He buried his face in his hands and slid down the wall to sit on the floor.

Why couldn't she love this man? He so obviously loved her with all his heart and soul. He'd never disappoint her. He'd always be there for her. *What's wrong with me?*

"Casey, I promise you, I'm not pregnant. Your mother is wrong. I'm still a virgin. I swear it."

He looked up at her words, his face red and moist from tears. "But you love him, don't you Kat?"

She hesitated to answer, but he had to know the truth. "Yes, Casey, I do." She stood from the table. "I'm so sorry."

He looked back down, squeezing his hands together so tight, the knuckles went white. She'd crushed him again and for that, she would forever be sorry.

She started to walk to Casey, to comfort him, but he held a hand up to block her from coming too close. She had to make him understand she couldn't help herself. Her heart belonged to John even if he didn't want it. She was bound to John as surely as if she already carried his child. There was no reasoning with her stubborn heart.

She bowed her head in defeat. "I'll pack my things and leave right away," she said, quietly, swallowing back tears of regret.

The sound of a killed engine and booted feet hitting the sidewalk echoed from in front of the house. Two deep breaths later Katherine realized John stood outside the sliding door, lightly tapping on the metal frame. Relief flooded his features when he saw her standing there, unharmed and glowing. He carried a brilliant pink orchid and the dark, worried eyes of a man who cared.

The sorrow she felt only a moment before was instantly replaced by hope. He'd come for her. That was all that mattered.

~ ~ ~

Katherine walked slowly toward the open glass door, keeping her eyes trained on John's. She assessed him through the screen. His handsome face was haggard from lack of sleep. Relief danced in his eyes but his timid smile told her he wasn't sure she'd open the door. She wondered, did he come to fetch her because Momma told him to or did he really care?

The screen groaned as she slowly slid it open.

"Hello, Katherine. It's good to see you." He paused to look her over. "I brought this for you," he said, holding the flowerpot out for her to take. "I'm here to apologize for not standing up to your momma. That was my first mistake."

She accepted the flower, nervously fiddling with a delicate blossom, waiting to see if he had more to say. She wanted to jump into his arms and shower him with kisses, but she held back.

When she said nothing, he shuffled his feet. Waiting.

"She doesn't want to hear your apology. You don't deserve her. Why don't you go tell that crazy momma of hers she's never coming back? Just get in your fancy Jeep and drive away!" Casey stood behind Katherine, pointing a threatening finger in John's direction.

John didn't pay any mind at all to Casey's show but kept his eyes on Katherine. "Is that what you want, Katherine? Do you want me to leave?"

"Can you give me a second?" she asked John, and he nodded a yes. She placed the flower on the table and guided Casey into the kitchen to talk privately.

"What are you doing, Katherine?" Casey asked through gritted teeth. "Do you really want this guy? I know you don't want to go back to ranch life?"

"Casey, this is something between me and John. I don't know what's gonna happen, but I really need for you to understand, I have to see it through."

He pulled his hand away, anger dimming his eyes. "Well I don't understand. You do what you have to, Kat, but mark my words, you'll come back to me one of these days because I'm the only one who really gets you. He'll never be able to give you want you want. What you need. You'll see." He turned away from her, knocking the flower pot off the table as he stormed out the door.

"If you hurt her, I'll come looking for you. I promise you." Then he trotted across the street to the beach and disappeared into the waves.

"Oh my God," Katherine whispered to herself, working to compose herself before she faced John again. Casey's words sent shivers up her spine, but she'd hurt him. Again. It was her fault.

After a moment to regain composure, she found John leaning against the doorjamb, hat tilted down, hiding his beautiful blue eyes.

"So, do you even know what kind of flower this is?" She picked up the orchid and pressed it gently back into the plastic pot, thankful it wasn't damaged.

He pushed the hat back on his head to reveal the saddest eyes she'd ever seen. "Please say you'll come back with me? I don't know what's going on between us, but I can't get you outta my head."

Katherine's heart twitched with excitement, but her fear

of returning to the ranch held her. "I'm afraid to go back, John. I'm afraid of what Momma'll do."

"Trust me, she won't do a thing. I'll be right there to protect you. I'll never make that mistake again."

"So if that was your first mistake, what was your second?"

He shuffled his feet, then leaned toward her so his mouth was only inches from hers. "Not making love to you on that mountain," he whispered. "I've regretted it every single minute since then."

She felt a blush heat her skin when he pushed the hair back away from her neck and ran his warm fingertip along her jawline.

"Will you come back with me? Please?" His singsong voice was deep and brooding. Irresistible.

She looked up and smiled at him. "Let me get my things and thank Casey's mother."

His hand was warm when he took hers to lead her back to the Jeep. She was sad to leave Casey in such a mess, but hopeful John wanted her in spite of the terror Momma was bound to deliver on them when they got back home.

Chapter 22

Katherine and John rode in silence for nearly an hour. The chaos of traffic and horns gave way to natural beauty as they drove through Angeles National Forest toward the San Joaquin Valley farmland below. Her time to gather herself before the inevitable confrontation with Momma dwindled with each passing mile.

John cleared his throat before he reached across the seat to pull her in next to him. "You certainly know how to make an impression," he said, the playful singsong back in his voice.

"Can we talk about us before you take me home? I can't face her until I know where we stand."

He took the next exit and drove into the cotton field that lined the freeway. Dust settled as the old Jeep's engine sputtered to a stop.

"Before you say anything, do you think I might get a kiss?"

She squinted at him, confused that he could be so calm. "A kiss?" she questioned. "What's wrong with you? I thought you were afraid of me. I'm only eighteen, after all. Too young for you."

"Katherine. I want a kiss." He leaned over and took her face gently between his hands. He traced the line of her full, pink lips with his thumb, desire blossoming in his eyes. "I don't care how old you are. I just know I want you and if you still want me, we'll face the consequences together."

"You're not afraid of Momma?" She whispered, trying to remain calm even as her heart raced.

"Oh honey, I'm terrified of her, but I can't get you outta my mind. When you ran off before I could talk to you, you scared me to death. I'm sorry I acted that way at dinner that night. I was afraid your Momma would have me thrown in jail for lusting after her little girl." He smiled when she looked up at him in surprise.

"She might yet." Katherine chuckled.

He scooted closer so their bodies melded together. "You think I might get that kiss now?" he asked again, his lips only an inch from hers. His strong arm felt like a sheltering tree limb around her delicate frame. Curious hands discovered the spots that made her sigh.

"Do you want me now?" She spoke the words between kisses. "This might be our last chance to be together before Momma kills us both." She wrapped her arms around his neck and pulled his mouth into hers.

"Oh yes, ma'am. I want you plenty. There's nothing I want more than to make love to you right here, right now."

Those words saved her life. She wasn't alone in the world anymore. She had someone of her very own.

Hunger took over as their lips met again. Desperation sizzled every place his skin touched hers. As he unbuttoned the tiny pearl buttons from the top of her dress, he placed ever more enticing kisses on the newly exposed flesh. She laid back against the seat and invited him to follow.

He pulled off her boots and socks first. His sexy blue eyes drew her in as he massaged her feet, then up her calves, and finally gently over the soft, tender flesh of her thighs.

"Oh mercy, your skin is so soft," he said, sucking in a breath when she wriggled at his touch.

He caressed her full breasts under the very dress she'd worn the first night they met. Searching. Exploring. Igniting.

She bit down hard on her lip when his fingertips danced over the lace covering her perked nipples. When his curious hands followed the curve of her hips, she instinctively lifted so he could cup her tight bottom and slide the white cotton panties down her legs.

The pressure of his thumbs kneading the tender skin of her inner thighs had her spinning with desire. "Ohhh, that feels so . . ." Her breath halted in her throat when his search grew ever closer to her aching center.

Every hair on her body prickled with need when he raised the dress away from her trembling body to see her for the first time.

"So beautiful." When he leaned in to place a gentle kiss on her thigh, she moaned again, losing all inhibition.

"You smell amazing." He inhaled the mix of lemon-scented perfume mixed with her growing desire. "Is it okay if I touch you, Katherine?"

She answered by scooting her body closer to him.

When he ran his hand up her thigh again, he found her warm and ready for him. "Mercy," he whispered, licking his lips. Gently, not wanting to move too fast, he combed his fingers through the thatch of dark red hair between her legs and felt her twitch.

"Oh, my," she said on an exhale, inching her body into his touch.

He curved his finger into her, kneading slowly at first, then more insistent as her breaths deepened. She writhed against the seat when a beautiful tingle began to build inside of her.

"That's it," he whispered when she cried out in ecstasy. He crawled up to bring his lips to hers, to feast on her, as he freed himself from his jeans.

She arched toward him when she felt him hard against her thigh.

"Please," she whispered, capturing his soul with her pleading eyes. "I need you." The tingle turned to fire when he buried himself inside her. Once the sharp pain gave way to pleasure, she matched each thrust eagerly, allowing her body to relax around him. He bit his lip when he breathed her name. She unsnapped the buttons of his shirt so she could feel his strong, muscled back flexing over her. His chest heaved with uncontrolled breaths. His sighs entranced her. He was a mythological god poised over her, all power and passion, just as he'd been on the back of that untamed stallion.

When she pulled him deeper into her eager body, he groaned. "You're a witch, Katherine Adams," he moaned, sucking in air, doing his best to maintain composure.

"A witch, you say?" She ground her hips harder into his. "I'll show you a witch." The musky smell of him along with their perfect rhythm brought on another round of ecstasy.

She cried out, shivering through yet another orgasm. "Can we do that again and again?" She tossed her head from side to side as the tantalizing vibration washed over her.

"Absolutely." He took in a few deep, centering breaths. "Come up here with me, baby." His gaze devoured her.

He sat back against the long bench seat and pulled her up to straddle him, still hard inside of her. A mess of wild auburn silk danced around her face. When she realized she had full control, she threw her hair back and smiled an evil smile. His eyes went wide and watchful when she tugged the dainty blue dress over her head and tossed it to the floorboard with the last bit of her innocence. The lace bra was quick to follow.

"You're all mine now." She licked his lips seductively. Gripping the back of the seat, she glided her body up and down against his, instinctively knowing what would drive him crazy. Her plump breasts bounced inches from his mouth.

"Oh my god. Just look at you," he whispered again. While he massaged the tender flesh, he ran his tongue around each silver dollar nipple, suckling until they drew into tight, delicious nubs.

Her head fell back as another orgasm rushed over her body.

He didn't stop this time. He met her thrusts and let her ride the wave until he could hold back no more.

A flock of crows picking at bugs on the ground outside the Jeep fluttered away when he let out his cry of release. He collapsed against her chest and nuzzled there to catch his breath.

She kissed his hair and over his forehead, taking in his manly scent. His skin tasted salty and delicious.

"I think I love you, John Lattrell," she whispered as he held her tight against his warm body. "I hope that doesn't scare you off."

He didn't move his head away from her to answer. "I ain't going nowhere, young lady. You're stuck with me now, like it or not." He buried his nose in her hair and inhaled. "Nowhere, indeed." He let out a satisfied breath.

She lifted his face to hers, their eyes diving into one another's soul. "But do you love me?" She prayed she hadn't misread him completely.

"With all my heart," he answered as he kissed her chin. "What do you think about us getting married before going back to the ranch? Then your Momma won't have a thing to say about it. And if she does, we'll pack up your things and leave."

Katherine perched her lips against his, letting his proposal run over in her mind. "I think that's a fine idea. Mrs. John Lattrell does have a ring to it." She grazed her lips over his, then kissed him more demanding, until he was ready inside of her once more.

The trip home would have to wait a little while longer.

Chapter 23

It took Katherine and John two days to find a justice of the peace to marry them. Each moment, each adventure brought them closer together, stopping along the way to make love and reassure one another this was the right thing to do. They'd almost convinced themselves they were invincible until they pulled up the long drive at Ruby's Ranch to see Momma on the porch, hands on hips, angry beyond any time Katherine had ever seen.

When Stan saw the dust waft up under the willows, he rushed from the corrals to run interference.

Katherine had only been gone a few weeks but it felt like a lifetime. She'd lost her virginity, found the love of her life, experienced the big city, and became a wife all in a short expanse of time. All she had to do now was make Momma see her as an adult instead of her little girl. That was going to be quite a trick.

John hopped out of the Jeep and ran around to open Katherine's door. She stared at Momma, there on the porch. So menacing. The dogs rustled around, doing their best to break the ice. Momma hadn't moved one inch since they first saw her as they came up the drive. Her piercing eyes threaded over Katherine, most likely trying to understand where she'd gone wrong.

"Thank you, John, for bringing Katherine home where she belongs," were the first words out of Momma's mouth. Not the expected why, when, what happened words, but words of appreciation.

Confused by her momma's uncharacteristic calmness, Katherine rocked back on her heels to rethink what to say next.

John, thankfully, responded. "You're most welcome, Miss Rube. Your daughter is very important to me. I wanted her safe as much as you, I assure you."

Momma's eyes moved from her quivering daughter to John. "Oh really, young man? How could that be? You barely even know my daughter. How could she be that important to you already?"

Katherine looked up from the ground where she'd been staring, concerned John had stepped into something he wasn't prepared to handle.

"We're in love, Momma," she blurted out, interrupting her next question. "And we're married!"

Stan made it to the porch just in time to catch Momma as Katherine's words registered. He guided her onto the porch swing, then ran to fetch a drink of water.

"Young lady." Stan's eyes went dark. He huffed at Katherine as he rounded the door, holding the glass. "Just what in the hell are you trying to do? Can't you see you've already frightened your momma half to death, running off like that? Now you blurt out you're married? Are you trying to kill 'er? You know better."

He sat the glass on the porch rail and patted sweat from Momma's forehead with his handkerchief.

A flash of regret nipped at Katherine. She didn't want to hurt Momma on purpose, but she had to protect John. She wouldn't allow him to be abused by the same hand that spent years trying to quiet her. It wasn't going to happen. She straightened her shoulders.

"Stan, it's true. We're married and we're in love. If Momma can't accept it, we'll pack my things and move on. I'm sorry if it hurts ya'll. It wasn't our intention."

Stan looked to John for reason. "She telling the truth, son? You two get married?"

John stepped forward, removed his hat, and placed his arm securely around Katherine's shoulders. "Yes, sir, it's true. I know it's fast, but I love 'er."

Katherine melted a little inside when she heard him admit he loved her. She was secure and wanted. Momma's wrath couldn't touch her anymore.

"Mercy. This isn't what I meant when I said do whatever you have to do to bring her home, son." Stan shook his head.

"I wouldn't have come home at all if not for John, so don't blame him." Katherine looked Stan in the eye.

A long pause followed as each of them contemplated what to say next.

Stan shook his hand and waved for them to move away. "Why don't you kids go back there and check on Buckshot? Cricket's been fidgeting like crazy since Kat's been gone. I need some time with Rube. Go on now." He helped Momma to her feet and led her into the house. Mumbling.

Katherine didn't know what was being said between them but she knew if anyone could talk Momma down it would be Stan. John took her hand and led her to the back corrals.

"This could get ugly," she warned him.

"Don't worry about me, sweetheart. I've seen plenty of ugly in my life. My guess is she won't do anything to run you off again. You're her little girl." He brought her hand to his lips and kissed the tiny gold band he'd placed there, for better or worse.

That vow was about to be tested.

Chapter 24

Thirteen Years Later

Tiny laugh lines reflected back at her from the antique mirror as Katherine combed through her long, auburn hair. She didn't mind the threads of silver that now laced coyly through the curls. Her skin still glowed, and her figure still had the bounce of a younger woman so overall, the years had been kind to her.

She and John had conceived their first child the day they made love in that cotton field. Casey's mom had predicted a baby on the way and they'd made her prophecy come true.

Their little girl, Ruby Marie, was named after Momma who had calmed a great deal since Katherine had her own family to tend to at Ruby's Ranch. Seven years later, they welcomed a quiet little boy named Jake into the family. Lucy, a beautiful chocolate lab puppy, was a gift from Stan to their growing family. "No little boy should grow up without a faithful dog by his side," he'd said and he was right. They'd become fast friends.

Ruby Marie was her daddy's shadow from the start. She rode alongside him on horseback, learning to love the life of a rancher like no little girl should. Katherine understood her daughter's need to be close to her father, recalling the precious times she spent under the sun and sky with Daddy. Ruby Marie was a strong-willed, brave young woman who would always be able to find her own way. Katherine was proud of that fact.

Jake was an altogether different kind of child. Studious and practical. He avoided taking unnecessary risks when none were warranted. He hated disappointing his father so much, he shied away from challenges and retreated into his books and bug collecting. John loved his son, there was no doubt, but he had no idea how to relate to him, which all too often caused him to snap at the boy. Katherine saw regret in John's eyes each time it happened.

Katherine couldn't think how to bridge the gap between father and son. She was helpless to save that precious soul from a life of ranching and helpless to make John understand there were people in the world who didn't thrive on the life he loved. But she couldn't hurt him. He'd saved her, after all. She loved him madly.

They'd hoped for more children, but John's riding accident had rendered him unable to father another child. He hid inside himself for months, feeling guilty and less of a man, but Katherine reassured him she felt blessed to have the two babies they had and he was more a man than any other she'd ever met.

Her children grew into independent, compassionate individuals right before her eyes. She cooked and painted and tended the small orchid garden John built for her. In that sanctuary, she recalled a time when all she wanted was to escape the life she lived at Ruby's Ranch, but now she couldn't imagine leaving the serenity and happiness it offered.

She laid the hairbrush on the dresser and sighed.

"Gorgeous, right?"

She looked up with a surprised jerk and met John's eyes in the mirror. He pushed away from the door frame where he'd been watching her and stood behind her.

"You may be biased." She closed her eyes and leaned back against his still flat stomach, loving the energy that passed between them.

"Let's go for a ride up on the mountain. You look like you could use a few hours away." John's singsong plea struck Katherine straight in the heart. The visit to the mountain and the shaman rejuvenated her every time. A few hours of alone time with John would definitely lift her spirits as well.

"That sounds nice." She opened her eyes and smiled a grateful smile. "You always have the best ideas," she growled.

He placed a kiss on the top of her head. "I'll get the horses ready. Grab a bottle of wine, and maybe some of those cookies you made this mornin?" He winked at her in the mirror and turned to go.

Her eyes sparkled as she watched him walk away. "I will. Just give me a minute to change out of this dress," she said, anticipation racing in her veins.

"Don't you dare," he called from the hallway. "It's sexy when you ride in a dress."

She smiled at herself in the mirror as the rosy blush of embarrassment colored her cheeks.

She grabbed an extra blanket from the hallway closet and called out. "Momma, can you keep an eye on the kids? John and I are going for a ride." There was no reply.

"Momma?" She listened for a response but none came. The door to Momma's room was cracked so she nudged it open, concerned. "Momma?"

In the dim light Katherine could see Momma sitting in her chair under a reading lamp in the far corner, scribbling away in her journal. The room was musty and stale, like a window had never been opened.

"Momma," she whispered again. The room closed in behind her as she made her way through stacks of books and discarded clothes on the floor.

"Oh my goodness, what happened to this room?" The messiness made no sense. Momma was always so meticulous with everything.

"What's wrong, Momma?" Katherine knelt down and watched as Momma worked to pull her attention from a distant memory.

It took a full minute for her to focus on Katherine's worried face. "He's gone," she whispered, slamming the leather-bound book shut. Uncharacteristic tears ran down her cheeks. "He's not coming back."

"Who's gone? What are you talking about?" Katherine reached to hold Momma's shaking hands.

Momma stood and moved away, attempting to pull herself together. "I don't know what I'll do without him."

Katherine followed, afraid she'd finally lost her mind. She'd gotten used to the occasional outburst, but this was different. "Who's gone, Momma? Daddy?"

"Augie. It's Augie. He won't come back to me anymore."

Katherine's brow furrowed. Augie was still with them, though his energy was noticeably missing from the disheveled room.

"What happened? Why'd he leave?" Momma's expression turned from fear to concern.

"His warning was about you. He told me to beware."

Momma tucked the journal safely in the chest of drawers, then wandered around the darkened room, collecting plates and cups in a stack to take back to the kitchen. She tidied as if she'd only just realized how cluttered the room was, then slipped away with an armload of dishes.

Beware, Katherine repeated the word to herself, looking around the room. It'd been years since the voice had warned her to beware. Was Augie the old man? Or the shaman? Or was he an altogether different soul? He'd been their protector so why would he leave Momma alone now?

Katherine shivered and left the room, closing the door on the chaos with a firm click.

When she joined Momma in the kitchen, she was her old

self, talking about what she'd like to make for dinner. Augie surrounded them both.

"I don't understand what's going on? Why is Augie in here, but not your room?"

Momma squinted at Katherine, questioning. She clearly had no idea what Katherine was talking about. "Honey, you and John go on your ride. I'll check on the kids. Don't you worry about a thing. You need to take care of your good man. They don't come along like him very often. If I were you, I'd hold on to him as tight as I could." She carried on, not addressing the question about Augie.

Katherine backed slowly away. "I'll get help Momma. I'll find out why he's left you," she said under her breath. She grabbed the blanket and ran toward the back corrals to escape the madness stirring in the house.

Stan caught her as she rounded the front corral. "Kat, what's wrong, honey? You look like you've seen a ghost."

"Please go stay with Momma. I think she's the one who's seeing ghosts." She breathed out. "I'm sending the kids next door to the MacCallister's. John and I are going for ride up the mountain to get some answers. Do you mind watching over her?"

Stan went pale. Without a word, he turned and trotted toward the house.

She hurried on to the corral. Her only hope of getting an answer was seeing the shaman as soon as possible.

Chapter 25

Katherine held Cricket's reins while John settled in on Buckshot. Over a decade older, the stud still sat a feisty saddle. John seemed excited to see the fire and interest back in Katherine's eyes but she was on a mission. She had to get to the mountain to find out what was going on with Momma. The answers would be found inside the circle.

She and John had barely reached the clearing before she slipped off Cricket and entered the circle. She drew a deep breath to calm herself, then closed her eyes and counted to ten.

The dance began as every other dance. The tips of her fingers stretched as far from her body as she could manage. Her shoulders made wide spirals as the shaman chanted. This time, instead of following him around the rock circle, she faced him.

"Katherine, don't," she heard John yell from outside the circle, still unable to join her in the dance after all these years.

She waved to assure him she knew what she was doing as she kept her stare trained on the shaman. He blinked against the directness, almost as if he was shy.

"What's going on with Momma? Why did Augie pull away from her?"

He stepped back and stood tall, wanting, she could tell, to speak directly to her, but he had no words.

"Talk to me, please. What's going on?"

She felt a physical touch from the vision when he held out the rain maker for her to take. *Take this.* The statement vibrated in her mind even though his lips didn't move. *It will guide you.*

Shockwaves rippled up her arms when the rain maker became solid in her hands. The beads rattled to the left and then to the right.

When the beads balance, your life will also become balanced. The more you struggle against your destiny, the louder the rattle will become. To bring balance, you must let go of things you cannot control. Only then will you find calmness and satisfaction in your soul.

"Augie?" she whispered, positive it was him. He'd been their guardian, their protector and now he was trying to tell her something important she couldn't understand. She had no idea how to achieve what he suggested or how any of this would help Momma through her crisis.

"What about Momma? Why have you pulled away from her?"

He shook his head, pain obvious in his otherworldly eyes. No explanations came to her, only sadness vibrated from him as he disappeared.

"Augie, she needs you. Please don't leave her," Katherine begged as he faded away.

A quiet whisper mixed in the wind when she fell to her knees. "*Beware, my child.*" The rain maker clattered loudly from side to side. Her life was completely out of balance, and Momma clung dangerously to the edge. Thoughts raged through Katherine's mind and into her heart.

How could she bring balance to their lives? To the ranch? How could she convince Augie to return to Momma?

Chapter 26

Katherine and John rode in silence back to the ranch. She was thankful he gave her the space she needed to work through Augie's words. Not that she'd accomplished anything.

As they descended Haley's Peak, Katherine spied a small red car parked in front of the house. It was no rancher's vehicle, she could tell. She prayed someone hadn't come to take Momma away. But she immediately shoved that thought aside. No one except her and Stan knew anything was amiss with Momma. And he wouldn't call for outside help. They'd take care of Momma's problems right here on the ranch. Like they always had.

"Get up," she called for Cricket to quicken her pace.

Buckshot easily fell into step.

"What have we here?" John nodded toward the car.

She shrugged and leaned forward in the saddle. Her hair whipped wildly in the wind as Cricket carried her at a full run.

Dust clouded across the porch as they reined in the horses. Momma's pale pink climbing roses covered so much of the railing they shielded the kitchen window.

Lucy sniffed curiously at the city tires on the red convertible. The personalized license plate, that read 1WILDRIDE, revealed nothing. The red leather seats bled into the carpet. The rabbit's foot hanging from the rearview mirror brought sadness and anger to Katherine's heart.

She looked from John to the half-opened front door then back again and frowned. Something sinister waited inside.

"Guess I better see what this is all about." She hopped off Cricket's back and handed him the reins. "You mind brushing her out for me? I'll be out directly."

He looked cautiously at the car, then leaned down for a quick kiss. "Go take care of your Momma. I'll be in when I'm done."

"Thank you, sweetheart." She smiled to reassure him though apprehension knotted in her stomach.

The smell of expensive, flowery perfume hit her the minute she stepped through the door. The fireplace room was eerily quiet and empty. When she rounded the corner to the kitchen, she caught sight of a five-inch red pump bouncing at the end of a long, slender leg. The hem of the black and white polka dot dress hiked high on shapely thighs.

By the time Katherine's gaze made it to the woman's face, all three of them—the woman, Momma, and Stan—stared at her in silence. The smile on the stranger's heart-shaped face was coy rather than friendly. She looked Katherine up and down, then whipped her long, bleach-blond hair back to reveal ample cleavage.

She was maybe mid-thirties. More trendy than sophisticated. Definitely not from around here. Her heavily-lined brown eyes were stark against the platinum of her hair. Long gold earrings and bangle bracelets clanged together as she repositioned to look Katherine over. Bright red fingernails tapped annoyingly against Momma's wooden table. The ruby of her lips made them look pouty, though she was obviously annoyed.

Stan squeezed Momma's folded hands then stood to walk to Katherine. The worry in his eyes told her this woman was trouble. She was not here for Momma, but for *her*.

Momma remained uncharacteristically quiet, her face pale. Her eyes festered with barely concealed rage.

The woman stood and glided in Katherine's direction.

"So, you must be precious Katherine? Aren't you a pretty little thing?"

Katherine waited a split second before reacting, half expecting Momma to fly up out of her chair to hog-tie the woman on the hardwood floor. But Momma's eyes only widened as her face reddened.

"I'm Katherine Lattrell. Who are you?"

The woman raised her thin eyebrows up to a point and pushed her hair back away from her face again. "Funny you should ask. My name is Sophie. Sophie *Lattrell*."

Katherine's mind spun in a hundred directions. "Lattrell? Are you related to John in some way?"

Sophie chuckled. "You could say that, honey." She seemed thoroughly pleased with herself.

Anger bubbled. Sarcasm irritated Katherine to no end and this woman oozed sarcasm with every word and every movement.

"You gonna sit there smiling like a fool, or you gonna come out with it?" Katherine took a step toward the woman, threatening. She wanted desperately to slap away her irritating smirk.

Booted feet hit the floor as Momma stood from the table.

"Sophie?" Terror crossed John's face when he saw betrayal bounce in Katherine's eyes.

"You know this harlot, John?" Katherine stepped back when he reached for her.

"Who are you calling a harlot, sweetheart? At least *I* didn't marry another woman's husband?" Her laugh was shrill.

Katherine felt her stomach plummet to her feet.

"I see. You didn't know. I guess you didn't bother to find out anything about John's past before you said, 'I Do'? He is quite convincing, isn't he?" Her voice was a sensual growl.

John's mouth moved but no words came out. Stan stayed as still as a statue, waiting for some cue.

"One day you'll listen to me, Katherine Ann." Momma's voice was low and raspy.

Tears didn't come to Katherine's eyes. Rage and frustration buried the hurt so deep inside, Augie swooped in to hold her heart safely in his hands before it shattered into pieces.

Beware, child. The words bounced inside her mind. For once, she understood their meaning.

"What are we gonna do about this little mess we're in?" The blonde seemed eager to have a discussion, but Katherine wanted out. She couldn't think. She couldn't breathe.

John reached again to grab Katherine's hand. She backed away. This lie cut too deep. Her sacrifices were too real. She'd given up her dreams to stay with him on this bloody ranch only to find out he was never hers to begin with.

"Leave me be, John," she spat.

The blonde smiled at him as she took a seat again at Momma's table. To avoid losing her lunch, Katherine ran out the kitchen door toward the back corrals. Away from the nightmare threatening her family.

What the hell just happened?

Chapter 27

Ray MacCallister answered the door wearing only a towel after Katherine pounded. His blond hair was wet from the shower, his muscular torso exposed and tan.

"Kat? What's wrong?"

Katherine stepped past him looking for her kids. "Where are Ruby and Jake?" she asked through her quivering lips.

"Hey." He turned her to look at him. "What happened? What's wrong? You look like you're being chased by the devil."

She lowered her gaze when tears stung her eyes. "I can't talk about it. I just need to get my kids."

"Nancy took 'em all to town to get ice cream. They left ten minutes ago." He put his arm around her and led her to the couch. "Sit down here and gather yourself a minute. Let me get dressed and we'll talk."

He disappeared down a hallway. After a long moment, he was back, Wranglers low on his hips, and pulling a Waylon tee over his chest. He settled next to her and put an arm around her shoulders. "Talk to me, honey."

Katherine welcomed his kindness. The usually crude and loud Ray MacCallister would've enjoyed being naked in front of her. This Ray was gentle and genuinely worried.

"Has John done something?"

She let go of the sorrow she'd been holding the second John's name was mentioned. The shoulder Ray offered in support smelled of fresh soap and deodorant.

"I knew that bastard was bad news when I first saw him.

I tried to tell you." He spoke under his breath as he squeezed her close. "So, what is it? What's he done?"

When she finally gained the courage to lift her head, he wiped the tears from her cheeks. "Come on, Kat. Talk to me."

"He's married, Ray. I mean he's got another wife. She's all feminine and fancy. She's sitting in Momma's kitchen right now."

Katherine felt him flinch as the words registered. "What do you mean, he's got another wife?" Ray stood and paced. "Was he married before you two met or did he marry her after?"

Katherine shook her head, realizing she hadn't found out even that much before she ran away.

"She's beautiful, Ray. Worldly. Everything I'm not."

"That son of a—" Ray's voice faded as he walked into the kitchen. Then he pressed a glass of amber liquid into her hands. "Here. Drink this. It'll help calm you down."

Katherine sipped obediently, then choked. "What is it?"

"Just whiskey. Finish it and I'll fix you some sweet tea, just the way you like it."

It took two more swallows, but she managed to get down the stinging liquor. True to his word, Ray soon handed her a tall glass of tea, so sweet after the harsh alcohol she nearly choked again.

After a few minutes, a warmth spread across her insides and the tightness in her chest loosened.

"Are you feelin' better, darlin'?" Ray sat next to her again and pulled her close. "Where did the woman come from?"

Katherine shook her head. "I don't know. She's so beautiful. How can I ever compete with that?" Tears streamed down her cheeks.

He tipped her face up to his and held her stare. "Kat,

there's not a woman in this world more beautiful than you. Get that straight in your head right now."

Then he kissed her, gently, on the lips. His lips were warm and reassuring against hers.

He laid her back against the couch and looked into her eyes. "I'm so sorry he hurt you, Kat," he whispered, kissing her again. Her eyes widened in disbelief when he pulled the T-shirt back over his damp hair and reached to undo his jeans.

She tried to push him away. "No, Ray. Stop. I can't—"

He caught her wrists and kissed each before pinning her hands above her head. Trapping her under the weight of his body, he pried her legs apart with a knee. "It's okay, baby. He hurt you. You deserve to hurt him back." His whisper was sinister. He'd switched from consoling to wicked just that fast and she was trapped.

She thrashed against his grip, but he was too heavy and strong to budge.

"Ray, get off me," she screamed into his insistent kisses, twisting her face away to catch a breath. "John will kill you!"

"Let's not talk about John." He licked his lips. "He betrayed you, remember? You know you were always supposed to be mine, Kat. You broke my heart when you married that asshole."

Panic rose when Ray hushed her cries, promising she would enjoy what he had in store for her. She tried to knee him in the groin when he lifted her dress and yanked her panties to the side, but it didn't stop him.

"Just relax, honey, and let me make you feel better. You'll never want John Lattrell again after you've had me."

She laid motionless and numb, unwilling to give him the satisfaction of her movement.

~ ~ ~

When he finally released her wrists and started to move off of her, she pushed him to the floor. Disgust crossed his face. "What'd you do that for?" He stood and grabbed her arm.

She kneed him in the gut and he doubled over. "As soon as I tell John what you just did, he'll kill you. You know he will." Her voice shook with rage.

Ray's face turned purple. "What are you talkin' about, darlin'? You practically begged for it. You came to me, upset about John. You wanted comfort. You wanted to prove you were as beautiful as John's *real* wife."

Katherine's heart grew cold. "You wouldn't."

His eyes gleamed with malice. "It's only the truth. Plus then everyone will know about us, including those precious children of yours. And your momma. You know she'll blame you, just like always." He licked his lips and smirked, satisfied he'd blackmailed her into keeping their dirty little secret.

Chapter 28

Katherine scrambled to get away from him. She had to think. How could she let this happen? Why would she ever trust someone like Ray MacCallister? She'd been so naïve. And now her whole life was in danger of falling apart.

Ray buttoned up his jeans but left off his shirt. He lit a cigarette and dropped into the winged chair, propping his bare feet on the coffee table. Smug.

She ignored him while she smoothed down the wrinkled dress and combed her wild hair with shaking fingers.

As she opened the door, he drawled a low, "Bye now, darlin'. You know where to find me the next time you want to get even with that SOB."

"You shut your mouth, Ray. I can't believe I trusted you." She exhaled a sob as Nancy's Land Cruiser came into view at the end of the driveway. Momma and Stan's silhouettes appeared at the top of the ridge.

Katherine rubbed her eyes and told herself to breathe naturally. She had to pull herself together.

The kids tumbled out of the car with a healthy, sugar fueled squeal, while Nancy got out more slowly, worry creasing her aging face. She stared suspiciously from Ray to Katherine, then to Stan and Momma who approached.

Katherine worked hard to stay composed. She avoided looking in Ray's direction, choosing instead to take each of her children by the hand.

"Time to go home, you two. Looks like you enjoyed your ice cream." She wiped the chocolate from Jake's cheek with her sleeve and kissed the top of Ruby Marie's head.

"Miss Katherine, does Ruby have to leave so soon?" Little Billy MacCallister asked as he stood at Ruby's side. His gentle eyes were innocent and hopeful.

"I'm sorry, sweetheart, but we have some things to take care of at home," Katherine answered. "She'll be back again real soon. Okay?" She bent down to tuck a wave of chestnut hair behind his ear.

"Yes, Ma'am," he agreed, unable to mask his disappointment.

Katherine smiled at the innocent crush Ray's little boy had on her Ruby. If only life could be that simple.

"What do you say, kids?" Katherine urged the kids to thank Nancy for letting them come over to visit, and for the ice cream treat.

Nancy smiled and kissed each of them on the cheek before glaring over their heads in Katherine's direction. "Your *children* are welcome here anytime, Kat, but I better not catch you alone with my husband ever again," she warned, keeping her voice so low only Katherine could hear.

Katherine blinked in surprise and guilt. Precious, quiet Nancy MacCallister had an assertive streak. "I-I understand," Katherine replied. "Believe me, it'll never happen again. I just came for my kids."

Momma stepped between the two women and guided Katherine off the porch by the elbow. When the door shut loudly behind them, she said, "I don't know what that was all about, young lady, but I pray you didn't just complicate your life even more."

Katherine ignored her mother. She smiled reassuringly when Jake and Ruby looked back at them. "Momma, I need to get my kids home and fed."

Momma pulled Katherine in and whispered so the kids couldn't hear. "You need to figure out what the hell's going on with that woman sitting at my dinner table before you march these innocent babies right into a mess."

Katherine stopped and looked at Momma again. "You mean she's still there? With John? Alone?"

Momma nodded. "We left when they started to argue. We were more worried about you."

"Jesus, Momma."

"Don't *Jesus* me, young lady. These are the kinds of things that wouldn't happen if you'd–a listened to me in the first place. People aren't always what they seem. You can't jump into bed with a stranger and expect everything to turn out perfect."

Katherine couldn't argue the point. She'd just thought she was letting an old friend comfort her, until it was too late. She had fallen in love with John without giving a thought to his past. She'd sensed he'd been around the first time they talked, but married? She'd never even considered that.

"I hear you, Momma," she said, her voice catching. "I hear you."

Momma put a comforting hand on Katherine's shoulder. "Stan and I will take the kids to the barn 'til you get this ironed out," Momma said. "You just holler if you need us."

New tears freshened in Katherine's eyes, thankful for Momma's support.

"Is Daddy okay?" Ruby Marie asked, sizing up with two older women.

"He's fine, honey," Katherine lied, not wanting to upset her daughter. "Just fine." She blew out a hard breath and prayed for strength to face the inevitable.

Chapter 29

John was gone when they got home. And so was the red convertible and the harlot that rode in on it. The note on the table read simply, *Don't give up on me, Katherine.*

She couldn't fathom any scenario, no matter how bad, that would take him away from the ranch, or away from her without some explanation. Why didn't he at least stay long enough to be sure she was safe? What would she tell the children? How could he leave with that woman? How could he be married to someone else?

The evening passed in a blur. She tended to her children, supervised their baths, and fed them, with her thoughts tumbling in her head like cut alfalfa in the thresher. Their children were illegitimate, their marriage a sham. And he'd known it all along.

She lied when they asked where Daddy had gone. "He's got a lead on a prized mare a few counties over," she'd said, hoping with all her heart that wasn't the case. Augie tried his best to hold her, to comfort her, but too many bad things all at once overwhelmed her ability to cope.

Images of John with the beautiful Sophie terrorized Katherine. But they were preferable to remembering what happened with Ray. Had she given him the wrong idea? Was Momma right, after all? That she was responsible for what men thought of her?

No. She shook her head. Maybe when she was a teenager, she'd enjoyed the occasional flirty glance or banter, but for the last thirteen years, all she'd spoken to Ray or Nancy about were cattle prices and who was picking up the kids at school.

By the time Katherine fell into bed, alone, she was too exhausted to thank Augie for his watchful presence.

~ ~ ~

Katherine entered the kitchen for the first time in days.

Momma stirred continuously to keep the vanilla pudding from sticking to the sides of the hot pan. Sliced bananas and wafers lined the bottom of her largest casserole dish. Fluffy, fresh whipped cream stood tall and stiff in the mixing bowl, with Momma's old two-pronged beater perched on its heel by the side.

"Banana pudding, Momma? Really? Are we celebrating?" Katherine's bloodshot almond eyes were so swollen, she nearly missed her mother's relieved smile.

Stan stood from his game of solitaire and took her into his arms. "Glad to see you, sweetheart. You gave us a scare." The scruffy hair on his unshaven chin tickled Katherine's forehead when he placed a kiss on top of her head.

Momma didn't respond or even watch the exchange, she just kept stirring. "Cricket will be needing some exercise, Katherine. She won't let anyone near her. You need to take care of it." She moved the pan off the fire, poured the hot pudding over the layer of cookies and banana slices and handed Stan the spoon to lick. "Stan, let Lucy in here to see Katherine's alive. She's been fretting somethin' awful. Following me around, whining. Driving me crazy."

Katherine melted to the floor when Lucy's wagging tail swatted around her knees. "Hey girl," she whispered to the giddy pup. She took her happy face between her hands and scratched behind her ears, accepting the sweet, wet kisses she offered.

"What a good girl you are." Lucy laid on the floor with her head in Katherine's lap and pawed for a belly scratch.

"Oh, I see what you missed." Katherine obliged as Lucy wrapped her paw around her hand to keep her scratching.

Stan sat in the chair next to them and watched. "That dog accomplished in one minute what we tried all week: Get you to smile."

The look of relief on his face made Katherine's heart swell. Stan did his best to be there when she needed him. She definitely needed him now.

"Still no call or letter?" she asked, reluctantly, getting to her feet.

Stan shook his head and looked away.

There'd been no word from John. He hadn't talked to any of the boys about what he planned to do. He packed only a few of his personal items, leaving his cologne bottle on the bedroom dresser. Katherine took it as a sign he planned to come back to her, but she couldn't be sure.

Ruby Marie and Jake spent most of their time with the MacCallister children, playing games and swimming in the pond. They were safe with Nancy even though Katherine, herself, didn't feel safe with her at all.

"I'll go tend to Cricket, Momma. I'm sorry I've been no help." She headed toward the door.

"Take that dog with you," Momma called after Katherine.

"Come on, girl." Katherine smiled when Lucy stood and shook. Her long velvety ears slapped hard against the sides her precious face. Her gold eyes sparkled with excitement. Lucy loved to torment the cattle in the back corrals. She was ready to have a run at them.

As she closed the door behind them, Katherine heard Stan admonish Momma for being cruel. "You need to hug your girl, Rube. She's hurting."

She didn't wait to hear Momma's response. She knew what it would be.

Chapter 30

If horses could smile, Cricket would've been grinning from ear to ear when Katherine walked through the barn door and opened her stall to let her out. Her huge brown eyes sparkled and assessed. Her head bobbed with excitement. The bond between horse and rider so strong, Cricket sensed Katherine's distress in an instant.

"I'll be okay," Katherine whispered into the long, soft ear when Cricket nudged her head against her leg to offer support. Tears stung Katherine's raw eyelids. She leaned into the mare and held tightly around her broad, strong neck. "I hope I'll be okay."

Cricket curved her long neck around Katherine's body as far as she could and held her in the only kind a hug she could offer. Lucy paced around the two of them, wanting to be included.

Katherine felt blessed to have the love and concern of these two majestic creatures. She felt safer in their company than with Momma, any day.

Cricket bobbed her head and walked the few steps to the equipment hanger. She nipped her bridle between her teeth and brought it to Katherine with a message. *Let's ride* rang out from the gesture as loud and clear as the shaman's words had before.

"Great idea, girl." In a matter of minutes, Cricket was fully suited with Daddy's old Western saddle and weathered split reins. Katherine pulled on the pair of working boots she'd left on the shelf and climbed aboard. Once they made it through the barn and out the corral gate, they were off and running. Lucy followed to the end of the fence, then turned back when she couldn't keep up.

Fresh air filled Katherine's lungs. She squinted against the brightness of the afternoon sun. When they reached the high corral, the cattle scattered from the pounding hooves. All but one cow moved away when she reined Cricket in to have a closer look.

The brave cow glared at Katherine, her helpless calf curled up at her feet.

Katherine always wanted off the ranch, but ranching and caring for the cattle was in her blood. She couldn't look away when she saw one of the herd in distress.

She hopped from the saddle and legged through the fence to check on the little calf. The lashes around the momma's huge, concerned eyes, batted hard with worry.

"What do we have here, girl?"

The cow calmed instantly at Katherine's soothing voice. She took a step away, as if asking for help. The rest of the herd watched cautiously from afar.

The calf lay flat against the grassy pasture as Katherine ran her hand along her coat. Just above the back left hock was bloody and swollen from what looked to be an animal bite. Most likely coyotes looking for an easy target.

She grabbed the first-aid kit from the saddlebag and hustled back to the injured calf. Daddy always told her to keep that stocked, because "someday you're gonna need it," and today she did. For the hundredth time since he died, he was right. She smiled in spite of her heartbreak.

When Katherine returned, the calf's mother had inched closer to nuzzle her baby. Animals do a better job at showing affection than humans. *There's a lesson to be learned in their every habit.* Her father's words echoed in her mind.

"Here we go, girl." Katherine knelt. "She'll be okay, Momma," she reassured the distressed cow. She squirted saline water in the wound, then wiped away the dried blood and debris from two large puncture wounds that had just missed the bone. The calf scuttled her front legs a little in protest but made no effort to move away. Momma cow mooed quietly against the calf's neck which looked to Katherine like she was helping hold her down so she could get doctored.

The wound was disinfected, covered in antibiotic ointment, and then wrapped carefully with gauze. The last step was giving the shot, but Katherine didn't hesitate. She tented the skin above the front leg and shoved the needle quickly in and emptied the syringe. The calf stood in protest and scurried off, stopping to look back when she was safely away from Katherine's reach.

"You're gonna be fine now, aren't you, girl?"

The calf studied her for a long moment, then turned back with her momma to join the herd grazing on the new grass that bloomed in the spring rain.

It felt good to help but it worried Katherine that the coyotes were coming in so close. She'd warn Stan when she finished her ride, but for now, she and Cricket were on a mission.

She knew where she had to go.

Chapter 31

The clover around the circle was covered in tiny white flowers. The air was cool and sweet with jasmine. The spring rains had washed the rocks clean so their symbols seemed freshly etched. The light glowed in the middle even before she climbed from the saddle and let Cricket roam.

The shaman's body began to form in the center of the light. His dark hair glimmered. Birds stopped chirping for a split second when he called out for her to join him.

Katherine stepped through the edge of the circle into the enveloping light. Rather than their usual dance, the shaman stared into her soul as if reading her mind. She felt sweet energy emanate from him. The weight flattening her spirit was pulled from her body as though it was being physically lifted.

She took a deep breath and exhaled heartbreak and worry, leaving hope in its place. He took her into an embrace, just as he'd done Momma all those years ago. It was as though God himself held her. There was no warning from him this time, only healing and love.

"Katherine!" John's singsong voice echoed against her mind. She didn't open her eyes for fear she would lose the connection with the shaman. But he let go.

The spirit stayed alight even when John entered the circle and frantically worked to get to her. She was still held securely in the luminous light away from John's grasp.

"Katherine, please?" John begged. "Look at me. Come to me."

She squeezed her eyelids shut and held tight to the shaman even as he tried to awaken her from the trance.

And then he spoke. "You have nothing to fear from this soul but you still need to beware."

Her eyes shot open. The shaman was now a man in front of her, his eyes a shocking pale green, like none she'd seen before. His touch strong, yet gentle, against her outstretched arms. He loved her, she could see, just as he loved Momma.

"Go, child." His lips moved with the words. She was awestruck that he'd come to life.

John wrapped his arms around her waist from behind and dragged her, unwillingly, away from the shaman. He'd doused the protective light so John could reach her. She didn't want to go.

The positive energy healed her. Her eyes no longer burned, nor did her heart ache. She stood tall and sure, her hair coiled and bounced with life. The shaman had renewed her energy, but there was still John's betrayal to deal with.

"Come with me, Katherine. Please sweetheart. We need to talk."

She wanted to be angry with him, but it was gone. The anger and betrayal had been drained from her.

"I love you, John. I'll always love you. If you tell me you're leaving me for Sophie, I'll feel blessed having had you in my life for as long as I have. We have two beautiful children together. I've been blessed."

John stepped back, eyes wide in shock. "I don't know what that shaman did to you, but I figured you'd rip me apart when you saw me. He must be some kind of a miracle worker."

She smiled. "He *is* a miracle, John. And he's shown me life's challenges are nothing but puzzles to be solved. I'm tired of being angry and hurt. It's time to move forward."

They stopped walking and sat on the clover. John pulled

his hat off and let it fall to the ground. "I was sure you'd never speak to me again after Sophie made such a scene."

"I had my doubts as well. Thinking you loved another woman nearly broke my heart. Especially that woman," she said, swallowing back tears.

John hesitated, then touched her hand. "There's never been anyone but you, Katherine. You own my soul. I'm so sorry I hurt you. That's the last thing I'd ever want to do." He looked away, ashamed.

"But you were married to her? Weren't you?" Her eyes dropped to the ground where she formed a tiny white bouquet from the clover flowers.

He took a deep breath, gathering his thoughts. "I did marry Sophie a very long time ago, but we got a divorce almost immediately after. It was a mistake. A terrible mistake."

Katherine didn't look up or say a word.

John stammered a little, then continued answering the questions stuck in her throat. "I met Sophie when she got banished to her uncle's ranch as a punishment. I was working horses for him and here comes this wild city girl looking to have a little fun with a ranch hand. I didn't know what I was doing. I was a dumb kid. I didn't even care she was messing with me to get back at her mother."

Katherine leaned down on to her elbow to watch him tell his story. So much could be discovered in his expressive blue eyes. She saw regret and embarrassment for the first time since meeting him.

He shook his head. "You probably think I'm a damned idiot, but we got drunk and run off to Vegas. I barely even remember saying I do. Even as I said it, I didn't mean it, but we were having a good time. Like most kids, I had no idea how one irresponsible decision would come back to haunt me."

She sat up and pulled his hand into hers. "Why didn't you tell me about her, John? Why would you keep this from me?"

"That time in my life was dead and gone as far as I was concerned. I was embarrassed that it even happened at all. I didn't see a reason to regale you with my ignorance." He brought her hand to his lips and kissed her fingers.

"So, you're still married?" She liked the way his lips felt against her skin even as she braced for his response.

"Not anymore. We went together and got it taken care of."

"So she was right, I did marry her husband." She pulled her hand away, a twinge of jealousy pinched in her gut.

He dropped his empty hand and looked down. "I thought it was a done deal. I signed the papers and she promised she'd take care of it. I moved on and she went back to the city. I never saw her again. End of story, until she showed up here and blurted it out. I'm sorry about her, Katherine. She's a spoiled brat. That's just how she is. Rude as hell."

"Yeah, she's a piece of work all right. Obviously a little hung up on you still or she wouldn't have been such a bitch to me." Frustration pounded against Katherine's heart, but she took a deep breath, reminding herself to keep the anger in the past.

"Evidently, she didn't realize the annulment didn't go through until she and her fiancée tried to apply for a marriage license a month or so ago. She finally tracked me to Ruby's Ranch. She's trapped herself some old, rich banker. Poor bastard. She wanted to get hitched before he came to his senses," he chuckled.

Relief filtered over Katherine as regret snuck in. She lifted his chin and smiled at him. "Well, I guess we have no choice but to move on from here then." She referred to her own terrible secret as much as his.

He blew out the breath he'd been holding and chanced a

look into her eyes. "Thank you for understanding. I thought I'd . . . I'd lost you." His voice faltered.

She touched his face. "What choice do I have? I love you."

Guilt filtered over her for a moment when she saw honesty and complete trust there. She opened her mouth to tell him about what had happened with Ray, but she shut it again. She didn't dare.

John would kill Ray. She knew that as sure as she knew the sun would set behind the hills. It would ruin so many lives. Swallowing her pain and humiliation was easier than taking the risk.

"You okay, sweetheart?" John reached for her again. Concern weighed down his already tired face.

She scooted next to him and brought his face to hers. "You scared me," she whispered against his lips before laying a gentle kiss there, tears of relief streamed down her rosy cheeks. "I thought I lost you forever to that fancy, city woman."

He ran his hand through her long hair to comfort them both. "That would never happen. I'm right here. I'm sorry for taking off without talking to you. I was so shocked I had to leave right then to make things right." He pressed into her. "I love you too, Katherine. With all my heart and soul. You're my life."

She had his shirt unbuttoned and untucked before he laid her back on the cool clover.

"Are you sure about this?" He whispered between kisses, anxiously nibbling her lips.

"Oh yes, I'm sure." She was desperate to feel his warm body against hers. Only this morning she was unsure she'd ever see him again. That made her want him all the more.

He followed the sensual line of her neck with warm kisses as he unbuttoned her shirt and worked to free her breasts. She shuddered when he took first one breast, then the other into his mouth, pinching each nipple, maddeningly, between his teeth. When he licked between her breasts, trailing his fingertip up her leg, she shook in anticipation. Even after all these years, his touch ignited her from within.

"Are you still sure, Katherine?" he asked, the singsong of his voice now laced with desire. When she said nothing he paused, his hand at the waist of her pants, waiting for his cue.

She raked her fingers through his hair and looked into his eyes to reassure him. "I want you, right now."

In a moment's time, her boots were off and her jeans thrown to the side. He stopped to gaze at her beautiful hourglass figure, still youthful after giving birth to two babies. Her breasts stood high as she laid back. She felt vibrant and whole. Undeniably feminine.

"How'd this happen? How do I deserve you? Look at you. You're stunning." He pinched warm kisses across her stomach, then over the tops of her thighs, holding tight against her hips as they moved toward him.

"Please, John. You've been gone too long." She begged him to douse the fire raging inside of her.

He leaned into her, kissing her sensually now. "Okay, sweetheart. Don't be in such a hurry. We have the rest of our lives." His muscular arms flexed when he tugged the shirt free and tossed it to the ground. His boots came to rest next to hers in a bed of soft clover.

Katherine was mesmerized as he stood to unbutton his jeans and slid them off one leg at a time. His chest and arms, strong and broad, his stomach a six-pack of muscle. He laid down next to her again to let her curious hands explore his body. He was so brazen and confident, every bit as sexy as the first time she saw him standing in the doorway of the town hall, if not more.

"Oh," he moaned, as she stroked the thin cotton fabric that held him at bay.

"You won't be needing these either, Mr. Lattrell," she whispered.

The breath caught in his throat when she slipped her fingers into the waistband of his briefs and tugged them down.

"Oh, my." She bit her lip, always impressed with his eagerness.

She kissed him, gently, then impatiently, her seductive stare trained on his. "I think you're pretty damn gorgeous yourself." Unable to wait even a moment longer, she rolled him on his back and straddled him like she would a wild stallion. She slid down on him, taunting him slowly then more insistently as his hips arched up to meet hers.

"Oh, sweet Katherine. You're still a wild one." He gripped her hips to slow the ride.

Frustrated, she tried to move again, to feel him alive inside of her, but he held her tight.

"Gonna be like that, huh? We'll see about that." She leaned down and rubbed her warm breasts against his chest, knowing it drove him crazy.

"Not fair." He sighed, releasing her hips to caress the soft mounds of flesh.

She nibbled his lips, her tongue now teasing. He rolled her over, holding himself steady inside of her. "Two can play at that game, my little witch." His strong, rope-calloused hand cupped her breasts as he matched her taunting thrusts.

"Oh, my," escaped from between her pursed lips as a familiar, delicious tingle spread through her loins. "I love you. So, so much," she moaned, sucking in long gasps of air as John moved sensually inside of her.

John gritted his teeth as he let himself go. "I love you, Katherine. More than you'll ever know." And then he collapsed next to her and held on tight.

"I've missed you," she whispered laying in his arms,

catching her breath. The birds flittered atop the trees above them.

"What's gotten into you?" He wound a curl of her hair between his fingers.

His heart beat loud against her ear. His deep voice vibrated through her body when he spoke. He smelled like leather and sex. He smelled like home. She closed her eyes and prayed this moment to last and for the world to stay at bay. But it wasn't to be as a strong breeze lifted leaves and debris into the air around them.

"What is that?" The smell of dirt enveloped them.

She sat up quickly when the wind whipped through the treetops causing the squirrels and birds to scurry to safety. A dark cloud of dust crept over the sun and blocked the light. "We need to get the kids and get home, John. Right now."

"Where are you going?" he asked in a groggy voice, half asleep. He reached for her but she was already on her feet searching for their clothes.

"Get up, we gotta get back. Dust storm's coming!" She pointed toward the horizon with panic. She half buttoned her shirt and quickly pulled on her jeans and boots, tying her long hair into a knot to keep it from whipping. "Looks like a bad one. We need to go help with the herd."

"Oh hell," John called out fully awake now, looking toward the growing darkness. He jumped up and pulled on his jeans. Buckshot and Cricket scrambled to them with a whistle.

Chapter 32

By the time they got the kids home and buttoned down the storm shutters on the house, Momma and Stan had most of the horses closed safely into their barn stalls.

Katherine and Ruby Marie piled cheesecloth sacks into buckets as John and the boys did their best to herd the cattle into the low pasture to shelter in the gully against the mountain. They had a better chance of survival if the high winds blew dirt and debris over their heads, even as the dust swirled in the air.

Every able hand wrapped scarves around their own faces and put on goggles to spare their eyes before preparing their horses to ride. Cheesecloth sacks were tied over Cricket and Buckshot, Firefly and Jade's heads so they could see and breathe without taking too much sand into their lungs and eyes.

Three exhausting hours later the group had sacked each head of cattle to protect them as best they could. Instinctively, the animals huddled together and tucked their heads into each other's sides to shelter. If they made a sound, Katherine couldn't hear it through the roar of the wind.

When they rode into the corral, Katherine sent Ruby Marie in to check on her brother, while she led Cricket and Jade into the barn. The wind blew so hard it pushed her to the ground as she slid down off the saddle. Instead of scattering, Cricket and Jade stood strong over her so she could use their bodies as support to get back on her feet.

It took two men to hold the barn door open so it wouldn't snap off the hinges. Dust coated her hair, her face, around the line of the goggles. Sand that had blasted her skin fell from her clothes when she brushed them off. She coughed from the dust she'd inhaled.

The horses' eyes were flushed with saline then meticulously wiped with wet clean towels to remove the dirt and sand from their nostrils and eyes. Breathing in airborne particles, dirt and spores, can kill a horse faster than anything. She prayed they would all survive.

"I see you decided to come home to your family," Momma barked at John.

"Yes, ma'am. Always was coming back. Can't get rid of me that easy." He didn't look up from grooming Buckshot.

Katherine watched Momma run her angry eyes over John, spoiling for a fight. He didn't oblige and Katherine allowed herself one deep breath of pride.

"Looks like you brought hell back with you." Momma patted Firefly's rump which sent the mare trotting to the safety of her stall.

The wind howled through the rafters and slammed small rocks, tumbleweeds and God only knew what against the planked walls of the barn. The air was thick with dust.

Stan grabbed the remaining cheesecloth bags and headed back into the stalls. "They're gonna need these even inside. This is a bad one."

When he disappeared into the far stall, Katherine called after him. "I'll help." Maybe the distraction would keep Momma off John's back.

When she came back around the corner, she saw she was wrong. The distraction didn't work, but infuriated Momma even more. The boys had all disappeared from the barn, no doubt afraid to stick around. John was quiet and respectful, offering no excuses or apologies.

"I'd have to wonder about a man who'd be interested in that kind of woman to begin with," Momma kept on.

Katherine and Stan looked to each other before simultaneously taking a step to rescue the one they loved.

"Come on now, Rube. Can't this wait for another time?" Stan put his hand up to silence Momma's protest.

"We need to go check on the kids, John." Katherine put her hand on his back to nudge him along. "Momma, all this here is none of your business. It's between me and my husband, and we've worked it all out."

Momma moved Stan's hand away and sniped, "What husband, Katherine Ann? If that dreadful woman is right, you don't have a husband."

Katherine took a step back. It was true. She had no rebuttal.

"That's also none of your business. You need to concentrate on your herd of cattle getting beat down by Mother Nature right now. We'll be lucky if any of 'em are still alive when this storm's done."

Momma dropped the last of the damp cloths into the bucket and gave Katherine a cursory look. "No truer words have ever been spoken. You're right. We'll have to see what survives this storm, young lady. Won't we?"

Katherine understood her double meaning but stayed tactfully silent.

When she got no argument, Momma turned and headed through the barn door. "Come hold this damn door." John and Stan used all their weight and strength to maneuver the door against the wind.

Katherine covered her face again with the handkerchief and followed. Momma was right. Somehow, even after finding solace and strength in the circle, and rekindling her love and trust with John, she still felt danger looming all around her. Even the shaman had warned her so.

Chapter 33

John and Katherine brought their mattress into the fireplace room and pitched a tent using bedsheets to filter the dust. Ruby Marie and Jake huddled next to them for comfort and cleaner air to breath. Even Lucy found a spot at the foot of the bed to hide from the frightening storm.

The wind howled against the night, whistling like a giant flute across the top of the chimney and around the door and window frames. Towels were stuffed around every opening to the outside, but still the dust found its way in.

Jake shook in Katherine's arms, so she hummed every children's song she could think of to soothe his nerves.

"Daddy, do you think the horses will be all right?" Ruby Marie asked her father.

"I sure hope so, honey. That would be a tragedy if we lost any of 'em." He pulled the cover over his daughter's shoulder and tucked it in. "We're gonna have us a mess to clean up when this storm's over. We'd better get some rest."

But Katherine's mind raced. Surely she'd lose her orchids if the wind broke through the glass enclosure. And Momma's garden would be destroyed. Not to mention the cattle. Even if they lived through it, they most likely would be sick and weak. Perfect bait for those hungry coyotes.

"I forgot to tell Stan I doctored a downed calf up in the north corral today. It'd been bitten by a coyote or something. They're coming in closer and closer. Worries me."

John ran his hand over the top of Katherine's wet hair. "They ain't eating nothing right now. They're fightin' for their lives like the rest of us."

"Momma, coyotes scare me. They wouldn't try to get in here, would they?" Jake's little voice was so filled with fear, Lucy scooted up to lay against his leg.

Before Katherine could say a word, John answered, "No, son, they can't get in here. Even if they did, we'd shoot 'em before they got to us?"

Jake moved closer to Katherine's chest. "I don't wanna kill 'em, Momma," he cried.

"Oh come on, young man. You're gonna have to stick up for yourself sooner or later. If that means you have to shoot a coyote to protect your family, then you'll shoot it." John blew out a breath, frustrated that his son was so fearful and timid.

Katherine swept the hair away from Jake's frightened eyes. "Don't you worry, sweetheart. They won't come near us. We're just fine. You won't have to kill anything tonight. Daddy's teasing you." She pecked a kiss on his forehead and gave John a kick. "Don't torment him," she warned. "Ornery."

"You baby that boy too much, Katherine. He needs to learn to fend for himself."

"Well he's not going to fend for himself tonight. Let's just go to sleep," she whispered after a moment. She listened to the voice of the wind as it screamed its violent song.

Chapter 34

Morning broke with Katherine and Jake alone under the tented sheet. John and Ruby Marie had slipped out so quietly even Lucy still snored under the blanket.

Everything in the house was covered by an inch of dirt. The usual homey gingerbread and lemon scents of the house were overtaken by the smell of a freshly plowed field. Thankfully, the wind had stopped, but the sun strained to break through the dust still hanging in the air.

Katherine moved away from her sleeping son and tucked a pillow in her place so he could cuddle against it. There was no need waking him to see the disaster just yet. She wanted to be sure his collections were unharmed before he awoke. Lucy scooted next to him to keep him warm.

"Good girl." Katherine scratched the intuitive Labrador behind the ear then headed to dress. She had a lot of cleaning to do before she could even think about preparing breakfast.

The faces in the framed photographs on the mantle were almost unrecognizable. With the tail of her nightshirt, she wiped the dust away from her favorite picture of Daddy, taken only a few days before he died. The symbolism of dust covering his radiant, playful smile was not lost on her. She ran her thumb over the faded picture and remembered the night he died. That horrible, horrible night. The pain it caused forever etched in her mind.

Augie brought her into his embrace and held her there until the urge to cry subsided. She'd shed a million tears missing Daddy. She'd forever blame ranch life for his death.

"You don't have time for this, Katherine. Get busy," she admonished herself. She shook off the sadness and replaced the frame back in the niche of dust. "Love you, Daddy," she whispered. Then she placed a kiss on the tip of her finger and laid it against his smiling face.

"Okay, let's do this." She surveyed the rooms, each with a different level of need, thankful they'd been smart enough to close the doors to all the interior rooms, and stuff more towels under to keep them as clean as possible. The bathroom was virtually untouched by the storm.

After wiping down the counters and stove, Katherine whipped up a huge batch of biscuits and bacon gravy. She placed a serving of each in individual mason jars and closed the lids tight to keep the dirt out. She brewed two carafes of fresh coffee and squeezed a large pitcher of orange juice to wash it down. A simple hearty breakfast was all she could manage before more serious cleaning was done.

Katherine was terrified to go out to the barn for fear they'd lost their precious horses so she sent Jake out with breakfast instead. They piled the basket of food and drinks into the bed of his Radio Flyer wagon, along with a sack of wet washcloths to wipe dirty faces and hands. He was happy to help with Lucy right by his side. Katherine knew the bunch of them would work straight through if she didn't send food out. This was the best she could manage under the circumstances.

She pulled out Momma's prized Kirby vacuum cleaner and started around the windows. The dirt on the sills showed evidence of wide gaps between the square glass insets. The curtains and bedding were all brought down to launder and the walls brushed. The cherished knickknacks and maple wood furniture were dusted. She'd need help rolling Grandma's old rug up before she could see about cleaning the fireplace room floor properly but for the most part, the house was almost livable again.

Once she switched the laundry, moved the mattress back to the bedroom, and put on fresh linens, she decided it was time to face the disaster waiting outside.

She retied the beautiful climbing roses that lay puddled in a mess against Daddy's bench. Pots of Flanders poppies lay on their side, the bright red blossoms stretched long on their stems. The flourishing vegetable garden, blown flat, now resembled a barren field. It would take hours of careful, patient hands to salvage the plants with unsnapped stalks. That would have to wait for later.

Katherine timidly walked across the open driveway to see what remained of her precious orchid garden. Surprisingly, only a single pane of glass was shattered, the others intact. Half of the cedar siding lay scattered around the yard. The heavy metal roof with the misting system attached had been separated from the walls and set to the side as if a giant hand pried it off and dropped it there.

When she stepped inside, amazement flooded her. Shelves of untouched orchids greeted her, as if a force of nature sheltered them from the storm. Only two clay pots lay broken on the wood slat floor, the delicate white flowers brown with dust.

"What the devil?" She picked up the broken pieces and tossed them outside. "How did you all survive?" She blew the dirt off the blossoms and set the downed orchids in new pots.

"I guess we should've slept in here. Seems like it was the safest place to be." She replaced the scattered garden tools and set the rocking chair back on its runners.

Lucy met her in the driveway, all wags and happiness. Katherine sighed. If only she could be more like Lucy. Just glad to be alive and around the people she loved. The shaman had given Katherine hope with the intensity of his embrace, but she was drained after seeing the devastation laid on Ruby's Ranch by the storm.

"Katherine, honey, are you all right?" John's tired smile greeted her when she stepped back onto the porch. His boots lay filthy next to the bench, his muddy socks stuffed inside.

She raised her eyebrows.

"Figured you'd be out anytime, but you got me worried when you didn't come." His hands were the only clean thing on him.

She took him by the elbow and led him into the bathroom without saying a word.

"Where are we going? I need to run into town for some more supplies and medicine before they run out. We've got some sick animals."

"So, they're just sick? Or—?" She couldn't bring herself to ask.

"The horses seem fine. Stressed but so far, fine."

She dropped down to sit on the side of the tub and blew out a breath. "Cricket? She okay?"

"She's been whinnying like crazy, so we figure her lungs are just fine. She wants out of that stall though, I can tell you that much. If I didn't know better I'd say she's wanting to get out to make sure *you're* okay."

She smiled at him, thankful her Cricket was okay. "I'll put some sandwiches together and take 'em out to the guys. I'll check on her then."

"That'd be a fine idea." He leaned into her and gave her a kiss. "You're looking pretty dirty yourself. You interested in taking a shower with me?" His smile was wicked but his singsong voice enticed her as usual.

"I guess I could use a shower." She stood and dropped her dirty clothes to the floor, then helped him undress.

The warmth of his body against hers as the cool water flowed over them felt like their own private cocoon. Enclosed in the shower with the man she loved was the safest place she'd ever known.

Chapter 35

It took weeks to get the ranch back in order after the worst storm the valley had seen in decades. The cattle were slow to recover, coughing up dirt that had buried deep in their lungs, but they snapped back soon enough. By some miracle there wasn't a single casualty. Other ranchers hadn't fared as well.

The house took another three deep cleanings to finally erase all the remnants of dust from inside. The garden was another story. Tomato plants were snapped at the base and stripped of their leaves. Tiny granules of sand embedded in the tender skin of the fruit. Those were peeled and canned for cooking.

Some squash and melons were salvaged from under their leafy vines but the corn was a complete loss. To Momma's delight, all the strawberry plants were virtually untouched, sheltered beneath the protective netting she and Ruby Marie had made at the start of the season.

Everyone on the ranch pulled together in the aftermath of the storm, more thankful for each other and the many blessings of their lives. It could've been worse, Stan said. So much worse. But Momma didn't see it. She grew more frustrated and angry by the day. Katherine figured it was because Augie continued to stay clear of Momma's room, but she never asked.

With John gone to town for yet another supply run, Katherine decided it was a fine time to go for a ride with Ruby Marie. It'd been awhile since she'd had her daughter's undivided attention, so she took advantage. Jake hung back with Stan, decorating gingerbread men with his favorite candy sprinkles. Momma glared at Katherine, then walked off, muttering to herself.

Katherine sighed. Momma was getting crazier and unhappier with every passing day, but Katherine was at a loss what to do.

After saddling up Cricket and Jade, Katherine took the lead, with Ruby Marie close behind.

Bright orange and yellow wildflowers sprouted along the ridge in spite of the thrashing they'd endured in the storm. Nature was a powerfully restorative thing. Cricket and Jade did their best to stay on task carrying their riders, but now and again, they would bend in and nibble at the tender blossoms.

"Smile, Momma," Ruby Marie called out to get Katherine's attention. She'd snapped pictures of every living thing since she'd gotten that Kodak for her birthday. Katherine was one of her favorite subjects. She was happy to do it. It was the one thing that was their own.

Katherine pulled her hair back out of her eyes and waved her hat playfully in the air, for the photos. To see her daughter laugh and smile was reward enough. The air was thick with the scent of blooming sagebrush.

Cricket snorted, urging Katherine to move when she stayed still too long. She wanted to run, to head to the mountain and the circle where the tender clover grew, but Katherine didn't dare. Her daughter could never know about the circle, unless she was drawn there herself. She wouldn't push the family legacy on Ruby Marie.

"Momma, are you sad you never got to see Paris? Are you sad you never got to leave here?" Ruby Marie asked, not realizing the impact of that particular subject.

Katherine's heart squeezed in her chest at the questions. She didn't know how to answer without hurting her child, but she *was* sad. There was a piece missing in her life she could only see as Paris-shaped. Or art-shaped. What else could it possibly be?

Cricket stopped without any cue from Katherine. Her faithful horse expected her to answer her daughter's question.

"Sometimes, sweetheart, I still think about what it would be like to see the world. I admit I'm curious, but then I see how beautiful my family is, and how beautiful you are, and I count my blessings. I know I'm where I'm supposed to be." Katherine smiled to appease her daughter's concern.

Ruby Marie contemplated the answer for a while and offered, "You know you can still see the world and live here on Ruby's Ranch. You and Daddy could go."

She was proud, Katherine could tell, that she'd proposed a perfect compromise. "Wouldn't that be enough, Momma?"

Katherine smiled at her cleverness. "You're a smart one, you are. Yes, sweetheart. I suppose it could be. Maybe we will visit Paris someday. Maybe you can come with us?"

Ruby Marie smiled brightly at the idea as she walked in close to a grazing cow and snapped a photo right up close to the animals' curious brown eyes. Katherine was amazed at how agile and strong her daughter had become when she hopped back over the fence and on to Jade's back with ease.

"You wanna keep taking pictures or you ready to ride?" Katherine challenged.

"Ride," she answered with a competitive smile. She tucked the camera safely into the saddlebag and kicked into Jade's side. "Let's go, girl."

Ruby Marie stood in the stirrups and yipped loudly to urge her horse into a run. Katherine was content to bring up the rear but Cricket was having none of that. She whinnied her own version of the battle cry and kicked into another gear, leaving Jade and Ruby Marie in a cloud of dust.

Chapter 36

For the first time in her life, Katherine dreaded the annual barbeque at MacCallister Acres. Her one chance to dress up now seemed too dangerous a venture. There was Ray and Nancy to worry about and the constant talk of dead cattle on the lips of every rancher in attendance. But it wasn't to be missed. Momma nor John would've let her stay home.

Little Jake and Ruby Marie were the first to run through the patio gate in search of their friends and the special treat Nancy always had for them.

Ray's dutiful wife competed for the affection of Katherine's children. She didn't know if the poor, insecure woman did it intentionally or because she couldn't keep her man in line. Either way it was unnerving.

Every year was a little bit grander. With Ray in charge of the ranch now, everything was louder and more audacious. His dad, now semi-retired, sat back and enjoyed the first of several drinks, leaving the elbow-rubbing to his son.

When Katherine walked through the door on John's arm, Ray went silent mid-sentence. She stiffened and gripped John's elbow with white knuckles. She prayed he'd leave her be, but the dreaminess in his eyes was there for all to see.

"You all right, babe?" John patted her hand and she loosened her hold. "I'm fine."

Every day, every moment, she regretted that day she went looking for her children and ended up alone with Ray MacCallister. It would haunt her the rest of her days. Her heart thrummed in her throat remembering how vulnerable she had been.

"Ray." John stuck out a hand to shake before Ray could reach to take Katherine in his arms. "Looks like you and Nancy have outdone yourselves once again." Mentioning his wife didn't faze him at all.

Ray finally responded to John when Katherine looked away. "Yeah, figured since we all had such a shitty year with the storm, it might be nice to throw a real hoe down. Even brought in a buckin' bull for a little extra fun." He pointed to the mechanical bull set up on the far side of the patio. "I'll be looking for some action later."

Katherine could see Ray meant that as a challenge, but John thankfully, didn't bite. "Well, ain't that a hoot." John said, then guided her around Ray's wide shoulders.

"Kat," Ray hollered after them. "You look mighty beautiful tonight. All aglow." He winked at her when she glared back at him. "Aglow, indeed." His voice faded away.

Nancy watched out the window as Katherine and John walked by. They were a handsome couple. The best looking in the crowd of hard working ranchers. Katherine was at home and safe on his arm but her stomach lurched every time Ray looked her way.

"Why do you figure Nancy's still so jealous of you?" John asked quietly so no one else could hear. "She can see you're happily married, can't she?" He kissed her on the cheek and ran his fingers through her hair.

Nervous, Katherine shrugged. "She's hated me since we were kids. I can't tell you why. I've known Ray all my life. What can I do?"

"She doesn't like that Ray's always fancied you. That's what she doesn't like." John grabbed two glasses of cold beer from the make shift bar, handed Katherine one and took a sip from the other.

"Don't be fresh, John Lattrell. You know you're the only man for me." She sipped to hide her quivering lip inside the foamy head.

John sat down on a carved oak bench and pulled Katherine down next to him. He pointed across the patio at Ray. "Just look at 'im. Even now he can't keep his eyes off you."

Sure enough, Ray sat in front of the fire pit, surrounded by bargaining ranchers, one booted foot crossed on top of the other knee, his eyes trained directly on her.

John leaned over in front of Katherine and waved at Ray to break the spell. Ray waved back, without a care he'd been caught ogling another man's wife.

Katherine felt trapped between two lions. "I'm gonna go get the kids so we can eat. I'd like to get home before this gets ugly." She stood from the bench and smoothed down the sundress. "Here." She handed him the beer. "Drink this."

"Yes, ma'am." John's singsong voice teased as she walked away.

When Katherine pulled the slider open, Nancy blocked her entrance. "I'm gonna get my kids, Nancy," she said, meeting the woman's glare.

Nancy looked her up and down, disapprovingly. "They're back in Claudie's room. Playing. They're fine."

"It's time for them to come eat." Katherine pushed past her and headed down the long hallway. "Kids, it's time for dinner. Come fix your plate," she called, with no response.

Claudie's room was empty when she stepped inside. She looked twice to be sure they weren't hiding amongst the dozen stuffed animals covering the pink frilly bedspread. The room smelled of candy and powder, unlike Ruby Marie's, who preferred to fill her room with the scent of horses and leather.

Ray and Nancy's daughter was an odd one, but a good friend to her Ruby. Katherine felt a certain kinship with the girl. Ranch life didn't completely suit Claudie either.

Through the cross-paned window, Katherine spied Ruby Marie and Claudie telling high school girl secrets under a large live oak tree while nearby a group of rambunctious rancher kids played keep away with Billy's hat. Katherine smiled, seeing the adoring look spread across his face when Ruby jumped up to stop the game and placed the hat back on his head. He sure did have a thing for her. She wondered if Ruby Marie even recognized his crush.

"You lookin' for someone?" Ray's voice was barely a whisper behind her.

Before she had a chance to turn, he'd shut the door and pressed her against it. "You lookin' for *me*, Kat? Ready to get back at John, again?" He smelled of beer and cigarettes when he pushed his mouth hard into hers. "I've been thinking about you. I've been wanting you, Kat." His kisses, wet and sloppy all over her face, made her skin crawl. His hands grasped whatever flesh he could manage.

"Ray, stop," she yelled against his mouth, digging her nails into his cheek to push him away.

"Damn girl, getting a little rough, aren't you?" he growled, wiping away a droplet of blood. "You shouldn't-a left me hanging. You got me all worked up. You know I'm not a patient man."

A scream caught in her throat as he pulled her dress up and thrust his hand inside her panties. His body was so heavy against hers, she couldn't move.

When she tried to slide down to the floor he lifted her knees and brought her feet off the ground. With his mouth tight over hers to trap her cries, he ground his hips into her.

"Ray, you in there?" Nancy was outside the door, twisting the doorknob. "Ray, I know that's you. You get yourself outta Claudie's room this instant. People are looking for you."

Katherine was never so glad to hear Nancy's voice. One more moment, and Ray would've raped her again. She was sure of it. Tears trailed down her cheeks when he tried to kiss her tenderly now.

"Yeah, I'll be out in a minute," he answered Nancy, but he kept Katherine against the door.

A heavy sigh resounded from the other side of the door, then footsteps leading away down the hall.

"I told you I missed you, Kat," Ray whispered, licking his lips. His eyes were glazed from drinking and his cheeks bled from the scratches. He seemed genuinely surprised when he saw the hate and disgust in her eyes.

"You know you want it, Kat. Why are you playin' with me?"

She spat in his face and kicked him away when he sat her feet back on the floor. He backed away and arched a brow, confused. He ran his fingers through his slicked back blond hair, and wiped the blood from his face with his shirt sleeve.

"Feisty, aren't you?"

"No, you bastard. I'm not feisty. I'm disgusted. I don't want you. I never wanted you. How could you carry on with your wife in the next room? What is wrong with you?" She wiped her face with the back of her hand. "You stay away from me."

She opened the door and ran the few steps down the hall and locked herself in the bathroom to gain some composure and think what to do.

"Oh God, oh God," she said in a low voice. Panicked, she stared at herself in the mirror for a long time, thinking Momma may have been right all along. Maybe she did give men the wrong impression. She washed the blood from her fingernails and worked to put a fake smile back on her face. No one could know about this. No one. It would destroy too many lives. She would lose everything. Her family would lose everything.

When she opened the bathroom door Nancy stood stone-faced in front of her. The usual kind eyes she shared with everyone else were red and full of hate. They stared at each other until Nancy gained the courage to level her threat.

"If you don't leave my husband alone, everyone in this county will know what a tramp you really are. John and your kids will hate you. I'll ruin your Momma and Ruby's Ranch. Women in these parts don't abide by no whore running around with their men. You need to leave and never come back, Katherine. You hear me? Leave!"

Katherine could see Nancy was blind to the fact her husband was at fault. There were no words that would convince her otherwise. Her husband was obsessed with another woman. Did Nancy have the right to threaten her now?

"And the baby you're carrying, well, everyone knows it can't be Johns. You're a whore and everyone will know soon enough."

Katherine took a reflexive step back. She wasn't pregnant. She couldn't be pregnant.

Oh, God. Was she right?

It took every ounce of strength *not* to respond to Nancy. Someway, somehow, deep down Katherine felt it *was* her fault. Everything that had gone wrong stemmed from mistakes she'd made. The misconception Ray carried about her interest in him. Everything.

The tiny window of hope Katherine once held that no one would ever know about what happened with Ray now slammed shut into a haze of darkness.

Chapter 37

Katherine walked home from MacCallister Acres, feigning nausea. She was thankful the darkness and distractions hid her desperation. Momma and John were knee-deep in negotiations so it wasn't hard to pull off. She wasn't lying. Her stomach had flipped upside down the instant Nancy MacCallister confronted her.

John offered to drive her home, but she convinced him the night air and a nice walk was all she needed to feel better. That's what she told him but she had no idea what would really accomplish the goal.

She felt hopeless. There would be no winners. Life on Ruby's Ranch would never be the same. She couldn't trust it. Her terrible secret held her captive, forever afraid it would come out and hurt those she loved. But if Nancy was right, and Katherine was pregnant, it wouldn't be a secret much longer.

The leaves in the trees along the road rustled in the evening breeze. The scents of distant rain and alfalfa mixed around her doing their best to soothe her soul. The song of the country summer night was in full crescendo. Bull frogs croaked and crickets chirped. The whinny of a horse in the distance and the hoot of an owl, led the song.

Tears of surrender drained from her almond eyes, washing away what remained of her scant makeup. Her lips felt bruised where Ray had pushed his mouth against hers. The tender places he touched felt dirty and raw. Everything important to her was threatened. Momma's ranch. Her children's respect and John's love. It would all be gone.

Hoot. A loud screech echoed from an owl perched on the RR archway leading to Ruby's Ranch. The moon shined so bright above its head, it glowed shocking white.

He watched Katherine carefully as she approached. His bright gold eyes followed her every move when she stepped right, then left to be sure she wasn't imagining things.

"I suppose you have some message for me as well? I suppose you want me to *beware*? What else could I possibly beware of after all I've been through?" She stopped under the archway and looked up at the majestic creature who cocked his head at her questions.

"You needn't listen to the screech of an owl. I'm here to tell you. You need to beware." A familiar voice came from the darkness of the willows lining the driveway.

Katherine snapped back, frightened someone was so close without her sensing their presence. But the voice was so familiar and friendly. Teasing her.

"Who's there?" She took a bold step toward the shadows. "Come out and show yourself."

A chuckle came from the darkness. The chuckle of a longtime friend. She recognized it immediately.

"Casey? Is that you?" Hope flooded over her.

It was him, now a foot taller and shoulders half again as broad as when she last saw him in his mother's kitchen. His hair, now short, tucked into a perfectly fitted Stetson. He smiled his old playful smile. He was a man now, not a boy. He looked assured, where his younger self was always a bit timid. His hazel eyes sparkled when they came into the same light that set the owl aglow.

"Oh my God, Kat. Look at you. How did you manage to get even more beautiful?" He picked her up and kissed her on the lips before letting her slide intimately down his body.

Katherine stepped back and looked away from his uncomfortable stare, then brushed her dress back down against her body. Curiously shy for the first time in front of her lifelong friend. He was a ghost. A dream. He was so familiar yet a stranger.

"Everyone's at the MacCallisters," she said. "You know it's that time."

"I figured." His gaze gobbled up the sight of her.

She looked up at him, puzzled. "So why are you hiding here in the shadows? You should go over and say hi to everyone. JB and Dutch still work for Momma. And Stan would love to see you. They'll all be as happy to see you as I am."

"Are you, Kat? Are you glad to see me? Really?" A bit of the old insecurity peeked through before he could rein it back in.

"Of course, I'm glad to see you. I've missed you somethin' awful. You broke my heart when you left. Then that terrible way we parted at your mom's. We didn't even get to say goodbye. For the second time." She reached for his hand and squeezed. "Did you wanna pop over and say hi? I'm-I'm not feeling too well. I was actually headed home to lay down." She smiled weakly, trying to hide her disgrace.

"Kat, what's happened? What's wrong?" He tilted her face to the moonlight and grazed his thumb over her puffy lip.

She shied away.

"Who did this to you?" Casey's anger flared. His brow furrowed and his eyes glowed with rage. "Was this John's doing?" His voice raised uncomfortably loud.

"Shhhh, Casey please." Katherine turned to head up the drive. "Let's walk."

He quieted and fell into step with her as she walked toward the house. "So much has happened since I saw you. There's no good place to start."

"Start with who hurt you and work backward from there."

She accepted the hand he offered in support. She needed the comfort more than any other thing. Casey had held her through sadness, loneliness and heartache. He'd supported her when Momma embarrassed her and a hundred other ways throughout their childhood. It felt right to lean on him now when there was no one else to confide in.

"I don't wanna talk about that. At least not now. Can we catch up? What have you been doing? Why are you here?"

She looked around the front of the house when they reached the porch. "Did you walk here from Santa Monica? Where's your car? Horse?" It felt good to tease him.

He followed her to the door and graciously accepted the handful of gingerbread cookies she handed him. He didn't answer her questions and she didn't push. She didn't care at the moment. She felt safe with unconditional friendship.

They talked for an hour. He'd been here and there and everywhere. Loved a woman and left her, never finding the *one*. Always missing Katherine and the allure of family at Ruby's Ranch.

"I'm surprised you're still here, Kat. Honestly, I thought you'd have left a long time ago and followed your dreams."

Her eyes fell, giving away her own dismay at her surrendered dreams. "I love my family, Casey. I didn't lose my path as much as change it."

"That's crap, Kat. That's all you ever talked about for as long as I can remember. You were damned determined to leave here and look at you, married to a cowboy. If you were gonna love a cowboy, it shoulda been me. I still wish it coulda been me. It still can be, you know. I still love you. If he's beating on you, you need to leave 'im." He glanced at her swelling lip and clenched his fist.

She reached across Momma's table and took his hand. He was suffering and vulnerable, now a man confessing love rather than a childhood crush.

"You don't want me, Casey. Trust me. I'm a mess." She knew she spoke the truth. "Everything I touch turns to crap. The truth is, John is too good for me and my beautiful children would be better off without me." Tears freshened in her eyes.

"That's a lie. You're a dream come true, Kat."

The sentiment was lost when the sound of engines rumbled in the distance. "They must be headed back. Wait 'til they see you."

She was glad for the interruption. It was too intense, especially after the night she'd already experienced.

"I'm not staying, Kat. I don't wanna see anyone. I came to see you one last time."

"What do you mean, one *last* time? What are you talking about?" Panic rose in her throat. Her first thought was suicide.

"I-I don't know what I was hoping to find coming here, but I . . ." His voice faded away.

He stood from the table and pushed in his chair. "I'm leaving. You have a good life, Kat." He leaned in to kiss her cheek, then headed to the back door to escape.

"Casey, don't. Please. Please don't go. Can we talk? Will you talk to me?"

Headlights shined bright at the entrance of the drive. "I'll be in the circle tonight," he said. "Meet me there before dawn."

And then he was gone, jogging away from the house, up toward the back corrals with only the moonlight to guide him.

Chapter 38

Katherine planned to tell John about Casey but he fell fast asleep the moment his head hit the pillow. Instead she nuzzled against him. The rhythmic beat of his heart and the low growl of his breath soothed her. She loved the feeling of his strong, bare chest against her cheek. He smelled like home. Musk and soap and testosterone. He was all man. Her man.

She ran her fingers through the soft hair on his chest and was met with a low, sleepy whimper when she trailed down over his stomach. Even in sleep, the muscles flinched with her touch.

She wanted to wake him, to love him, but she couldn't get Casey off her mind. His return to Ruby's Ranch was more than an elusive homecoming, she could feel it. The way he watched her, measuring her. The way his heart broke with each word he spoke.

He knew about the circle. He'd told her to *beware* just as the spirits had always done. These were telling truths. Could he have some connection to the shaman? Could he answer every question she'd ever pondered about the mystical presence at the ranch? He was waiting for her now. If she didn't go she may never find her answers.

Katherine lifted her head and kissed John's chest. As she slid out of the bed, she laid another kiss on his hand before tucking it under the blanket.

She stood still and quiet while he shifted on to his stomach and punched the pillow under his head. Within a second, he quietly snored.

"I'll be back, sweetheart," she whispered. He didn't respond but snorted quietly instead.

She grabbed the dress she'd slung over the dressing chair and the boots tucked under her bed and slipped out the bedroom door.

The house was so quiet the tick of the kitchen clock kept time with the quickened beat of her heart. She pulled the dress over the tank top and panties she'd worn to bed and held the boots until she made it outside. She thought to take Lucy, but she would be nestled in with Jake for the night. She didn't want anyone to wake and ask questions. Casey would never talk to her if she wasn't alone.

Instead of riling the horses to take Cricket up the mountain, she ran across the pasture to the ridge. The moonlight guided her around the staggered herd, some dozing on their feet, others laying fast asleep on the cool ground. Quiet moos came from those she startled, while others seemed totally disinterested.

Tiny night creatures scurried away when she neared the rocks. Owls screeched from their high perches, and bats buzzed near the ground, nipping flying insects from the air. The night air was so crisp, Katherine regretted not grabbing something to shield her from the damp air.

The dewy clover squished flat beneath Katherine's boots. The meadow smelled of damp earth and jasmine. She stepped quietly around the thicket of poison oak toward the circle. A stream of light engulfed Casey who sat perched cross-legged on the center boulder, his eyes closed and forearms resting upright on his knees in meditation.

Katherine couldn't look away. He was mesmerizing. The shaman was nowhere in sight. Casey had somehow elicited the light without him. She couldn't figure how.

"Beware, child." The voice came from behind her rather than the circle. When she turned to seek the source, the voice sounded from in front of her.

"What, what?" Disorientation took over. The warning came from every direction. She felt dizzy and weak. She tried to call out for Casey to help, but she fell to her knees on the damp clover, her arms and legs unable to catch her when she hit the ground.

~ ~ ~

Katherine was alone when she awoke. She was no longer on the mountain, but somewhere she'd never been before. The bedsheets tucked tightly over her body restricted her movement. The loud beep above her head fell into a tedious rhythm. The needle slid roughly into her vein made her hand throb. Her mind was fuzzy, unable to form a clear thought. The mask over her face steamed calming, damp oxygen.

She must've been in an accident. Only that would explain how disoriented she felt.

With heavy eyelids, she fought to stay awake. Confusion didn't bother her as much as it should. She wasn't in a hospital, but an IV was attached to the needle in her arm. Her heart beat strangely in her chest. Instead of fighting against the confinement of the sheets, she felt safe in this strange cocoon.

She was alone, but not afraid. There was someone she missed, but she couldn't form the name.

Chapter 39

Nineteen Years Later

"Kat, wake up. Katherine, honey, wake up. Nap time's over."

The voice was familiar and soothing but her eyes wouldn't open.

"Wake up, sweetheart. You're gonna miss your opening. Come on, lazy bones. You've been working for this day your whole life."

The voice made her smile. But her head pounded so hard she was sure it would split in two.

His kiss was warm and inviting. His breath smelled of mint when he caught her lips in his. "You gonna get up or am I coming back to bed?"

She opened her eyes and returned his kiss. "I'll get up in a minute. I'm so tired. I need my medicine."

His sandy hair, touched with gray at the temples, was trimmed tight on the sides, slightly longer on top. Love and devotion oozed from his gaze. Age had only made him more attractive in a brooding, thoughtful sort of way. His broad shoulders were still defined and strong. His hands calloused from a life of hard work. The smile that spread across his lips was bright but ever cautious. Katherine loved when he shared that smile. It made him seem so mysterious.

"I had that dream again. The one with the horses. I don't remember ever riding a horse in my life. Where do you suppose these images are coming from?" Katherine held out her hand for him to take.

He watched her for a long moment before responding, as though he worked a problem through his mind. "Well, you're an artist. You have a great imagination. Maybe you saw a movie or something?" He patted her hand but looked away when she squinted in question.

There was much more to the dreams she couldn't explain. They felt so real, she almost expected to be wearing cowboy boots when she awoke. So many things she didn't share. Maybe she *had* taken in a good ol' western, or kept mental images from the thousand *Country Living* magazines she'd perused preparing for her show.

She brought her hand up to cover her eyes, squeezing her forehead up to relieve the pain. "I need my medicine. My head's killing me."

"Right away." He bounced up and walked to the bathroom. He brought back two small white pills and a glass of water she eagerly accepted. "Don't forget to do your breathing treatment, Kat. You want to feel good for your show."

She watched him walk confidently back toward the bathroom, naked and unashamed. The strong arms and shoulders that picked her up and held her. The still-narrow waist she'd wrapped her legs around.

He was everything a woman could want so why did she feel something was missing? There was a hollow place in her heart and in her memory. He'd said it was the amnesia from the accident that caused those empty spaces in her mind, but the blankness niggled at her every hour of every day. She could never quite reach the answer.

When the shower came on, she let herself daydream again. She rode a horse toward the sunset. Her hair was a stream of auburn fire. Her heart filled with love and family. The smell of jasmine and sage permeated the air. But it was only a dream.

The breathing treatments brought her back to reality. She couldn't function without them. It stopped the visions that haunted her and the sadness that came when they faded away. After she swallowed the pills, she took deep breaths from the mask hanging at the side of her bed. Instantly, she felt more centered and ready for her debut.

She'd finally made it. Her very own show. Painting was her passion. Sharing it with the world was her attained goal.

Katherine sat up on the side of the bed to gather her thoughts. She had to eat a little something to keep the nausea at bay, check in on Emma, and get herself prepped for the best night of her life. Feature artist at the New York City Chaucer Gallery.

She'd worked so hard, her blood and sweat covered the canvases. City people were eating up her visions of country life. Wildflower landscapes. Riders on horseback. Cowboys around a campfire. American Indians in a ritual dance. All pulled from the bedtime stories she'd made up to quiet her curious daughter.

"Mom, are you okay?" Emma peeked through the cracked door. "Do you need help with anything?"

Katherine patted the spot next to her on the bed. "Come sit with me a minute."

Emma, now almost twenty, was a stunning replica of her mother. Vibrant and curious. Kind and forever helpful. Just accepted into the nursing program at NYU. Her Momma's pride and joy.

"How are you feeling today, Momma?" Emma asked as she leaned her head against Katherine's shoulder.

"I could use something to eat, how about you?" Katherine kissed the top of Emma's head. Her shiny reddish-brown hair smelled of coconut and mint.

Emma looked up. "You feeling bad again? You don't look so hot."

"I'll be fine, sweetheart. I have to be. It's my big day!" Katherine lied. She felt awful. The years were catching up with her, the constant headaches and nausea taking their toll.

Katherine's vision blurred as she drank in the features of her daughter's concerned face. For a split-second Emma's smart bob haircut appeared to be a strawberry-blond ponytail. Her perfect pale skin became freckled. The NYU T-shirt she wore turned into a button-down riding shirt and her perfume turned to the scent of leather.

Oh, God. Katherine shook the image away. Her hallucinations were getting worse, but she didn't want Casey to know. He worried so much already, he barely let her out of his sight. Even the art show was billed under a different name to protect her from stalkers.

"Enough worrying about me. How are you feeling, sweetheart?" Katherine asked, ever concerned her daughter's seizures would come back as mysteriously as they had stopped.

Emma smiled wide and said, "No more episodes. They're all gone. Besides, I have no time for that. My momma is a famous artist. We have to celebrate."

Tall shelves lined with flowering orchids covered the off-white dining room wall separating the small kitchen from the living area. It took up far too much of the precious space in their small apartment, she knew, but she loved them.

Casey joined them at the tiny dining table which looked out over the bustling SoHo street. Harry's Bar on the corner stayed open twenty-four hours to fuel the neighborhood drunks. Vida's yapping Chihuahua, Peppy, barked at them from the balcony next door.

"Hello, Peppy," Casey called before closing the balcony doors. "Damn he's a pain in the ass." He sat down and filled his plate with fruit and imported cheese from the deli downstairs.

Katherine smiled across the table, handing him the loaf

of French bread and filling his wineglass with a dry Chianti. "He's lonely. Animals don't belong cooped up in the city. They need to be out in the open so they can run."

Casey's eyes shot up, nervously. "Indeed."

Katherine wasn't sure why she'd even said it but she saw it bothered him, so she changed the subject.

"Do you think I should cover the gray in my hair before tonight?" she asked, looking from Casey to Emma, tugging at a strand of hair.

Emma shook her head from side to side, chewing. She swallowed, then added. "I like it natural, Momma. It's very sophisticated. As a matter of fact, I think you should let it grow long like the lady in your stories."

Casey looked up from his plate and laughed nervously. "Stories?"

"Yeah, I miss your stories, Momma." Emma reached for a drink of Katherine's wine, which she quickly moved away.

His face went white. "What stories are these, Kat? Maybe you can tell them to me sometime?"

She smiled to calm him, tucking the strand of hair behind her ear. "Bedtime stories for a little girl, Casey. Nothing more."

"Momma, stop. I loved those stories."

"I'm sure I would, too. I can hardly wait." Now his voice was a growl as if he was being backed into a corner. He downed the remaining wine in his glass and pushed away from the table with a loud scrape. Fidgeting with frustration and nerves for no reason.

Katherine reached for his hand when he walked by, unsure why he was upset again, but he was already two long strides away.

"I'll be back for you both in an hour. Be ready to go. I have an errand to run."

He was out the door and down the stairs before Katherine could respond.

Chapter 40

When Casey returned to pick them up for the show, he was star struck by their beauty. Katherine wore a long, form-fitting charcoal gown, with flowing layers of chiffon down the back. The garnet earrings and a pendant choker set off her eyes.

Emma was just as stunning in her emerald-sequined knee length gown. Pewter stilettos accentuated her shapely legs. A rope of silver hung to her navel.

They were a vision.

The anxiety drained from Casey's face when Katherine kissed him tenderly on the lips. "You like?" She twirled around for him to see.

"You're beautiful, Kat. You're both beautiful." He looked from one to the other. "I'm a lucky man."

She enjoyed the compliment for a second, then realized the time. "Now, hurry up and put on your fancy monkey suit so we can go."

He carried a small bag with him into the bedroom to change. She thought to ask what it was, but there wasn't time.

Casey was a perfect match for her when he walked through the door in a double-breasted navy suit with a charcoal tie. He held out his hands and bowed. "Will this work?" He winked playfully.

The wink triggered shuttered images inside Katherine's mind. The picture of the debonair Casey replaced by a man sitting astride a reared black stallion. His electric blue eyes winked when he smiled. And then he was gone and her heart ached at the loss. Those eyes. She knew those eyes, but how?

"Oh, God. What's wrong with me?" Confused and frustrated with knowledge just out of reach, she felt faint and weak.

The image of the handsome cowboy burned into her mind.

The niggle came over her again. Who was this man? "I need to sit for a minute." She dropped down on the nearest chair and clutched her face in her hands.

Casey and Emma rushed to her, Casey on his knees in front of her, Emma rubbing her shoulder.

"Kat, what is it? What's wrong?" Casey's genuine concern comforted her though she kept the image to herself. "I'll get you more medicine, Kat. I got something stronger to stop these hallucinations. You sit there quiet for a few minutes." He got up and trotted toward the bedroom.

"Emma," she whispered with a quiver in her voice. "I think I," she stammered, watching down the hall. "I think, I can't be sure, but I think those stories I told you might be real. I think my memory is coming back and I don't think they're *stories* at all. Shhh, don't say anything to Casey until I sort this out." She kept her voice low.

"Why don't you tell 'im? He'd be so happy. Maybe he could tell you if they're real, couldn't he?"

"I've told him some over the years, but he says it's only my imagination. I don't know. Every time I bring it up, he gets nervous and gives me more medicine." She shook her head to clear her mind. "Help me up, sweetheart. I need to get up. Don't say a word to Casey. Not a word. Promise me? I need to figure this out without his help."

"Yes, ma'am," Emma agreed. Tears of concern rolled down her pink cheeks. She looked too upset and worried to ask questions.

With Emma's help, Katherine stood up on her four-inch strappy heels, feeling wobbly still. When Casey returned with two more pills and a glass of water, she dismissed herself to the bathroom. "Thank you." She half smiled. "Let me freshen up and then we'll go."

She felt his eyes on her the whole way down the hall. Mumbled voices talked of her illness, she was sure, but she was also sure of another thing. She would never discover the truth behind the visions if she continued to erase them with drugs.

Katherine didn't recognize herself in the bathroom mirror. It was her face, but her soul was missing. The circles under her eyes had darkened more and more over the years. Her hair was more gray than auburn. The makeup she'd used to hide her flaws only highlighted the confusion she felt.

She flushed the pills down the toilet, then turned again to her reflection. "It's time to take hold of this, Katherine. Even if you're going crazy, let's get on with it." She drank the water from the glass, placed it carefully on the counter and headed out the door.

"Shall we go? My audience awaits." Katherine feigned composure. The last thing on her mind was the opening, even after spending much of the last twenty years taking classes about color and design, texture and depth. Hours of practice and pain to finally make it to this point. The more realistic her paintings became, the less real her life became. She only saw it now.

A smile of relief crossed Casey's worried face as she walked to him. Her steady gait and squared shoulders gave the illusion of confidence when she was more uneasy than ever before.

She'd trusted him for so long, it was hard to think he might be hiding something from her. With all her heart, she prayed her intuition was wrong. She prayed he hadn't deceived her all these years.

"Are you feeling better, Kat? You ready for this?"

She looked up into his worried eyes, then ran her finger along the scar on his forehead.

Wondering.

As hard as she tried, she couldn't remember the story behind this scar. Wasn't this something a woman should know about the man she spent her life with? Why couldn't she remember?

"Yes," she lied. "As ready as I'll ever be."

Chapter 41

Her paintings depicting country life seemed strangely out of place hanging in an uptown gallery. The stench of the street and the bustle of the cars, only steps away from beautiful flowers on the range, didn't seem right. The mumble of fashionably dressed art enthusiasts fawning over each piece sounded like bees over sweet orange blossoms. The banner above the door read, *Country Life—A Dreamer's Perspective. The Chaucer Gallery welcomes Artist Jordy Mattson.*

Jordy Mattson, where on earth had Casey come up with that ridiculous name? But she'd let him do it like she'd let him make every other decision for her. Like some kind of zombie. Until now, she'd never questioned his motives. He kept the distractions away from her painting time and her special time with her daughter. It kept her from questioning the missing pieces.

Claire, the smartly dressed gallery curator, rushed to her when they made their quiet entrance. Katherine instantly dreaded what was about to occur. Everyone in the room would be curious about her. They'd want to know more about her muse. She had no answers for them. Or for herself.

She had no past she could recite to them when they asked about her inspiration. No life experiences bled onto the canvas. Only her daughter Emma to show and Casey, the man she was only now realizing she didn't really know.

Where had she grown up? Did she have siblings? And parents, what happened to them? How could she not care to know these details? Was Casey that great at deflecting her curiosity all these years or had she even bothered to question. Why couldn't she remember? Anything?

"Excuse me, everyone, can I have your attention? This is our special guest, talented artist Jordy Mattson. Please give her a nice welcome."

A rush of people clapped as they gathered toward her from all around. They'd expect her to say something clever. But no words came to mind. Maybe something like I have no idea who I am or where these images came from. She was sure that would never do. She swallowed the rising panic.

"Thank them, Kat. That's all they want." Casey stood behind her, whispering directions in her ear.

Katherine smiled a fake gracious smile and held up her hand to silence the applause. "It's a great privilege to hang my paintings in the hallowed Chaucer Gallery. A dream come true. I hope you enjoy yourselves this evening. I know I will."

She grabbed a glass of champagne from a passing waiter and held it up in salute. "A special thank you to everyone who's helped me along the way, to Claire and Chaucer's for believing in me, to Casey and my Emma for encouraging me, and to all of you for being here tonight to help me celebrate my special night."

After they drank, they mingled. Ears were perked to comments from the onlookers. Katherine tried not to eavesdrop but they were critiquing her heart. It was hard to deny she hoped for positive reviews.

Casey smiled at her. "How're you holding up?" He handed her a glass of water with a thin slice of cucumber floating on the top. She'd never seen salad mixed in a beverage but she gave it a try.

"Tasty." She frowned, picking out the cucumber and eating it. "I wonder if they have any tea hiding back there? That sounds better. Do you mind, sweetheart? I'm sorry to be a pain."

"I'll go check."

"Casey?"

He looked back.

"With lots of sugar, please?" She made a funny face and held her hands together in prayer.

He stared at her, his eyes darting around the room. He walked back to her so he wouldn't have to yell. "Kat, you don't use sugar in your tea. You never have. Are you okay?" His voice rose with the question.

"Really?" she asked, frowning as if he was mistaken. "Well, I think I might like it. Do you mind?" She pecked him on the cheek. "I'll be over with Emma." She pointed in her daughter's direction.

~ ~ ~

Katherine was right. She loved sweet tea. It was nectar for humans. Before she knew it, she'd emptied the entire glass and asked for another.

"Momma." Emma laced her hand through Katherine's elbow and led her toward the painting of a man on a reared black stallion. The same image that had flashed in Katherine's mind earlier.

"There's someone with a question about your *Man of Passion* painting. I think he wants to buy it." Emma giggled like a child. Excited for the success of the show.

"Can I help you, sir?" Katherine held out a hand to greet the patron.

He stood a slumped six-five. Maybe late-seventies with a little paunch hanging over his large silver belt buckle. A dark tweed blazer with leather pockets and collar corners buttoned over pressed Wrangler jeans. His skin was red and blotchy from too many hours in the sun. He wore a five-thousand-dollar Stetson Diamante and handstitched alligator boots tipped with silver. His rope-calloused hand felt rough and right in her hand.

"Well, hello, Ms. Mattson. It's right kind of you to come talk to me. I know you're a busy lady. Looks like these paintin's are flying off the walls." His southern drawl was playful and teasing, with a singsong tempo.

She felt the heat of a blush cross her face. "Well, I don't know about *flying* off the walls, but it seems city folks appreciate a little country, after all." The cadence of her voice matched his.

"I'd have to agree." He turned to the painting and pointed. "I was wondering where you might-a come across my nephew? Looks to be a long time ago but I'll pay you ten thousand dollars for this painting right now if you can tell me where I can find 'im. We lost track a good while back and I'd sure like to reconnect."

Katherine's eyes widened and she rocked backward on her spiked heels.

He braced her elbow to steady her. "Oh, little lady. You wouldn't wanna fall off those stilts. You'd surely break a leg."

"Did you say *your nephew*?" Black horses and blue-eyed riders flashed in her mind. His warm smile so familiar.

"Yes, ma'am, that's John all right. I'd recognize him anywhere. Not many can hold on when a bronc goes vertical." He pointed to the reared horse in the painting. "And this here. You captured his features perfect. I mean perfect. Just look at that. It looks like a picture. How on earth can you do that?" He smiled, amazed. "The telltale is those eyes though. Just like his Momma's. Shocking blue."

Katherine listened intently as he described the subject in the painting as a real, live man. She hadn't considered those eyes or that face had come from anything else but her vivid imagination. But she couldn't deny the images flashed in her mind. Where'd they come from? How did she know this handsome cowboy?

"What did you say his name was?" Emma asked the question on Katherine's over-stressed mind.

"That's my Johnny. John Lattrell. My sister's boy. Ain't no doubt."

John Lattrell? John Lattrell? His name was a song inside Katherine's mind. How'd she know a John Lattrell?

"I-I don't remember. I'm sorry." Katherine stammered, reaching for memories beyond her grasp.

"Well, you listen here. If you figure it out, you give me a call." He pulled out his hand-tooled leather wallet and fumbled for a business card. "This here's my personal number. Call me anytime." He closed her fingers around the card and patted her hand. "Call me if you remember. Or . . ." he said, stalling, ". . . you call me if you have questions for me." He held her tight with his concern.

"I will." Tears bubbled in the corners of her eyes.

"In the meantime, I'll be wanting this painting. I'll talk to that pretty little curator over there. You look like you might need to have a seat, darling." He wrapped his arm around her back and nearly carried her to the half circle couch at the entrance of the gallery.

"You take care, honey. You'll figure it all out real soon. I'm sure of it."

She wanted to call after him when he walked away, but she didn't dare. He'd think she'd lost her mind. And Casey would surely stop her questions before the cowboy had a chance to answer. She clutched the business card to her chest and prayed for strength and clarity.

Chapter 42

The next morning, she only pretended to inhale when Casey gave her the mask. The pills he'd handed her were flushed down the toilet the moment he left for work. She watched him exit the double doors downstairs into the street before she rifled through the bathroom cabinets to find the medication he'd been giving her for years. How could she be so trusting?

The bottle of pills had no label. No doctor's name or prescription. The small white pills had no number or description etched on them at all. The sack of powder he'd used to fill her breathing machine was tucked into his medicine bag buried under rolls of toilet paper. It read *Devil's Breath* on the small tag inside the plastic bag with the warning written in red. *Beware, may cause amnesia, confusion, hallucinations, unusual thoughts, headaches, nausea, agitation, and blurred vision.*

She covered her mouth in shock, her heart raced and tears welled again in her eyes. "Is he trying to kill me?" Katherine sat on the floor of the bathroom and shook her head in disbelief. How long had he drugged her and why? If they were in love, if they were a family, why would he want to hurt her? Was he drugging her when she carried Emma? "Oh dear god." The thought of him endangering her sweet daughter caused her heart to shudder. Guilt rained over her for not protecting her child.

Tears rolled down her face. Her head pounded. Her morning meal sat at the top of her throat. The realization angered her and terrified her all at once. Devastated her.

What was he trying to hide from her? What could be so important he'd endanger her and Emma, the two people he professed to love so much? What had she forgotten? *Who* had she forgotten?

She rubbed her face and ran her hands through her hair, trying to force her mind to open. "Please," she whispered, hoping she'd gotten this all wrong. She'd lived a full life with Casey, raised Emma together, but could it all be a lie?

And then the name blew back into her mind like a warm wind. John Lattrell. John Lattrell. She repeated the name over and over in her mind, and then out loud, hoping it would trigger a memory.

She was careful to tuck the drugs back in exactly the same place, then washed her hands of any residue. He couldn't know she was suspicious. If he had gone to this length to have her, what would he do to her, and to Emma, if he felt them pulling away?

On her way to the gallery, she stopped at the corner bakery to order a coffee to try to settle her growing nausea. The smell of fresh-baked gingerbread hit her when she pushed open the glass door. Every other time she'd passed through that door, she smelled hot sweet bread or doughnuts but today gingerbread was on the menu.

"Are those cookies I smell?" she asked the heavy woman behind the counter. "They smell heavenly."

"No cookies today, but the bread is just out of the oven. Would you like a sample?"

"Oh, yes, please." Katherine felt like a five-year-old with her hands pressed to the glass case of a candy shop.

The small piece of dark brown bread steamed from the paper container. A tiny plastic fork stuck in the middle. She laid the fork to the side, pinched off a corner and placed it on her tongue. The flavors mixed together in her mouth and in her mind. As the bread dissolved, so did pieces of the barrier that held back her memories.

She remembered willow trees, and the iron RR at the top of an archway. She remembered the name Rube Adams, her mother. She remembered Ruby's Ranch. She had children and John Lattrell was the love of her life. With every chew, a new memory emerged.

"Can I get a loaf of this to go, please?" She washed the piece down with the tears in her throat.

"Of course, doll. I'll have it right up."

Katherine pinched another bite off the bread and remembered standing in the kitchen, baking sheets of gingerbread cookies. Momma sat with Stan at the table, talking over the spring drive.

"Oh, God," Katherine said out loud to the stares of the other patrons. "Oh, dear God." Tears choked in her throat as memories began to unravel in her mind.

She ran as fast as her feet could carry her back to the apartment. "Emma," she yelled trying to catch her breath. "Oh God, Emma." Tears nearly drowned her as she fell to the floor.

"Momma, what is it? What's wrong?" Emma fell to the floor next to her mother and held on tight until Katherine could form the words.

"We gotta leave. Right now," Katherine told her. "Pack only what you can't live without and do it quickly. We have to get out of here before Casey gets home."

Emma sat up, fear straining her eyes. "But, Momma, he loves us. Why would we leave him?"

"Because he's the devil, Emma. The truest devil I've ever known. Go pack. I'll tell you all about it after we're gone from here."

Emma was speechless, tears in her eyes, shaking her head. "Momma, Casey wouldn't hurt us," she said through a whimper.

"Trust me, sweetheart. He would do anything to keep his secrets. Now go pack. We've gotta get out of here."

Katherine scampered to her feet and packed the only suitcase she'd ever owned. Shoved some essentials into the makeup bag, along with the money from her gallery sale and pulled her reluctant daughter from the apartment.

She had to find them. She had to know what really happened. How did she come to be under Casey's spell? Why hadn't they searched for her? Did they still want her after all this time? What did they think of her? Did they think she ran away and left them? Had they ever wanted her at all?

Chapter 43

All during the cab ride to the airport, Katherine filled Emma in on the scattered pieces she remembered so far. She could almost hear the questions going through her daughter's mind. Had her mother found a passage to her lost memories or had she gone completely mad? No matter the cause, Katherine knew Emma would stick by her side through it all. Even against Casey. Especially against Casey, if he'd done this unthinkable thing.

They were on the first flight to California. By a stroke of luck, the plane was boarding right when they passed through the gates. Katherine was desperate to get away before Casey came home from work. Waiting their turn on the runway, she used Emma's cellphone to dial the number to Ruby's Ranch she'd easily accessed from information. A man she didn't recognize answered the phone so she disconnected without saying a word.

"Why'd you hang up, Momma?" Emma asked.

Katherine looked down at the phone in her hand and smiled a wry smile. "Can you imagine getting a phone call from a ghost?"

Emma thought before answering. "I suppose you're right. We'll be there soon enough. We'll get this all sorted out, I promise. Don't worry." Emma took the phone from her mother, switched it off and stowed it in her purse.

"I can't face Momma 'til I talk to John." She looked out the window as Emma squeezed her hand.

"Momma, I don't want to think it, but," she paused. "What if John's gone?"

Katherine hadn't thought of that. He could be dead.

"I'll find him, Emma. Now that my mind is starting to clear up. I have to find him. He can't be gone. I need to shed light on what has been dark for so long."

Katherine's head pounded and nausea rose when they got to cruising altitude. She didn't know if it was a reaction to flying or withdrawal from the drugs, but she prayed for something to give so she would feel halfway decent when she arrived at Ruby's Ranch. She would need all her strength and energy to face the thousand questions that were bound to come.

"Here, Momma. I got this from the flight attendant. Maybe it'll help." She handed her a couple of aspirins to swallow and a warm, wet cloth to lay over her throbbing eyes. It soothed her instantly.

"Thank you, sweetheart. I hope your Granny Rube is as generous when we walk in her front door."

Emma settled in against Katherine's shoulder and held her hand. "Tell me about Granny Rube, Momma. I wanna know everything."

It dawned on Katherine that Emma was completely in the dark about life at the ranch and all the people there. The only things she knew were distant visions from childhood stories and the few scattered memories she shared on the cab ride over. Emma had a brother and a sister, and a crazy grandmother to boot.

Her heart pounded and squeezed with the pain she'd caused John. Such a good man, a good father. The love of her life was left behind with no way to know what happened to her. What if he thought she wanted to go? What if he didn't believe her?

Casey had been clever. The details were still fuzzy, but she did recall long hours of restless sleep in the back of a motorhome as it rattled down the road. With each mile and each pill and each puff from the mask, she lost more and more of her life until finally she remembered nothing at all but the man who was with her and the baby on the way. A baby that could very well have died from the assault of drugs coursing through her body. He'd convinced her she'd lost her memory in a bad accident. That's why she couldn't remember. Her distain for him grew with each breath.

Casey had convinced her that he was there to save her, to pick up the pieces of the life he destroyed. It was so easy to trust him. She knew he hadn't meant to hurt her but his sin was unforgiveable. He kept on, even after he knew she was with child. He kept on to serve his own selfish need to keep her with him.

He must've been desperate. Katherine worked her mind over, searching for an excuse, a reason, he would be so cruel. His mind was never right after the accident. Before that fateful night when they crashed into the ditch, he would never have gone this far. He would've loved her from afar and let her go, but never this. This was evil.

When he slammed his head against that steering wheel, he lost that kindness, that sweetness. The moral barrier that we are born with was ripped away. If she wouldn't come to him on her own, he would erase her life and make her love him. And he'd done just that.

"You okay, momma?" Emma asked, interrupting Katherine's distressed thoughts.

"Your Granny Rube is a strong woman, Emma. She was rough on me growing up. My childhood was totally different than yours. She had a plan for me. I was to become a rancher, to take over the helm when she stepped down. Not that she'd ever do that. That ranch was her life. Her world. I was a responsibility to her growing up. At least that's how I felt."

Emma laced her fingers into Katherine's hand. "She couldn't have been that bad, Momma. She raised you and you're a great mother. A kind person."

Katherine smiled beneath the cool cloth. "I'm glad you think so, sweetheart, because I have a feeling we're gonna run into a lot of people who think differently about me. Twenty years of absence can wreak havoc on relationships. My Ruby Marie is a grown woman. My Jake probably has a family of his own. They were kids when I was kidnapped. I'm not sure they'll ever forgive me. They may not even remember me."

"Of course they'll remember you. We'll make them understand, Momma. What Casey did was a sin. I know he did it for love, but it was wrong and I'll never ever forgive him. He had no right."

Katherine removed the cloth from her eyes and surveyed Emma. She was her baby but she was wise and insightful. Her heart was as big as the ocean. She must've done something right to raise such a giving soul.

Katherine's stomach rose in her throat when the plane made the final descent. They'd land in Los Angeles and make the two-hour drive to the Kern River Valley. A trip back in time. A world away from New York City and the life she'd led for the past two decades.

Chapter 44

A person could learn a lifetime of information from one trip to a small-town drugstore.

Katherine drew in a deep, regretful breath when she discovered she was too late to fix things with Momma. She was gone. She died alone a few months back with only Stan by her side. Her search for her missing daughter had never ceased.

The family split not long after Katherine's disappearance. Heartbreak and accusations forced John to pack up their children and leave the ranch. After losing her only daughter, then her beloved grandchildren, Momma fell victim to depression and isolation. At least that's what the town gossip said.

All the pride and control Momma once wielded could do nothing to restore her family. Not knowing if Katherine was alive or dead brought on the kind of madness only a truly loving mother could feel. The cloud that always hung heavy over Momma's head had swallowed her whole.

Katherine was proud Momma had seen fit to leave the ranch to Ruby Marie. That child loved the ranch as Momma always had. She was the one true matriarch. The rightful owner. Only in her hands could the legacy live on.

Martha said Ruby Marie arrived home not so long ago and had done wonders updating the house. She'd infused life and hope back into Ruby's Ranch and the faithful hands that kept it going. Stan was so happy to have her home. It made losing Rube just a little less awful.

Her precious John now lived in a care facility in Colorado Springs. His mind fell victim when his heart shattered into pieces. If the circumstances were reversed, Katherine knew she, too, would have lost her mind. In a way, she *had* lost her mind.

When Katherine and Emma came upon the spot where she'd first seen the shaman in the road all those many years ago, she started, half expecting him to appear once again. A second later, she remembered what else had happened along that road and even before.

Tears filled her eyes as she recalled the horrible night of her abduction. The thought of Cascy stepping out of the darkness twisted at her heart, but the memory of Ray—and the rape—came to life like a nightmare. Emma. Oh God. Emma. She was Ray's child. A child not of love, but of violence. How could this gentle young woman come from such hate?

"Emma, can we stop here? I need to tell you something. Something I just remembered." Tears ran freely down her worried face.

"What is it, Momma?" Emma looked at her with concern as she pulled the car to a stop along MacCallister's irrigation ditch.

"What's wrong? Tell me." Emma took her mother's hand and pulled it to her.

Through her sobs, Katherine attempted to guard her child's untainted heart. "I always told you I didn't remember who your father was, because of the accident."

"Yes, Momma. The amnesia erased all those memories. Casey said my real father never cared enough to find us." She went silent and passed her mother a tissue from her purse. When she caught Katherine's eye, she asked quietly. "Momma. Do you remember who my father is? Oh, please say it's John." Hope danced in her voice.

"Oh God, forgive me," Katherine cried, covering her face with the tissue. "It's not John. It can't be John. Your father has to be Ray MacCallister. I grew up with him. That there is his place." She pointed toward MacCallister Acres up the road.

Emma's eyes were wide and shocked when Katherine finally gained the courage to look at her. "But you were married to John. I don't understand. Did you have an affair?"

Katherine was amazed at how mature her young daughter had become, no doubt from living in the city instead of sheltered on a ranch as she'd been.

She shook her head. "No sweetheart, I didn't have an affair with Ray. He—" She squeezed her daughter's hand. "I want you to know something first. I want you to know I love you with all my heart and nothing in this world could ever change that. You are my precious gift."

"Of course, Momma. I would never think anything different. What's wrong? Why are you so worried?"

"Because he raped me, Emma. Ray raped me. Oh god, honey. I'm so sorry," she shook her head in regret. "I shouldn't have told you. It serves no purpose for you to know because I couldn't love you more, even if you were John's baby girl."

Emma opened the car door and stepped out, taking in deep breaths. Gathering herself, trying to wrap her mind around what her mother was trying to tell her.

Katherine jumped from the car to rush after her. "Please, sweetheart, you have to understand. I should've known better than to trust Ray. He took advantage when I was upset and vulnerable. I'd only just realized I may be pregnant when Casey snatched me. As much as I prayed for a miracle, I knew you couldn't be John's child."

Emma turned when Katherine stopped walking. "How can you be so sure?"

"Because John couldn't father children after his awful riding accident. There was no doubt."

Emma looked down and kicked at the dirt.

"I was petrified to tell John what had happened with Ray because I knew he'd go after him. I couldn't hurt my family." She looked up into her daughter's understanding eyes.

"Momma, please. None of this was your fault. You can't keep this to yourself. It's too much to hold inside."

Katherine sniffled. "When Casey kidnapped me and started with those drugs, my family was ruined anyway. I could kill him for putting you in danger."

Emma raised her eyes to meet Katherine's, assimilating the reality that came along with her disclosure. "The drugs could explain my seizures. Maybe a side effect?" Emma said more calmly than she should.

"Oh Emma. What did I do? My pathetic need for attention could've killed you." She sobbed into her hands, too devastated to even look at her daughter.

Emma peeled the hands from her mother's guilt-ridden face. "No one deserves what's happened to you, Momma. There's no behavior in the world that gave these men the right to do what they did. None." She kissed the delicate, paint-stained knuckles. "Please momma, don't blame yourself. We will figure all this out together. We need to find John. We need to bring you back to your fairy tale and everything will get sorted, I promise."

"You're an amazing young woman. You're so much braver than I ever was. I don't deserve you."

Emma paused and watched as Katherine's mood began to lighten. "So," she finally asked. "Did you ever punish Ray for what he did to you?"

Katherine dropped her eyes to the ground again, ashamed. "I kept it to myself—to protect everyone and everything I loved. Revenge wasn't worth the price. It was easier to swallow my pain."

"It wasn't easier, Momma. I don't care if he is my father, he needs to pay for hurting you. No man should get away with that." Emma stood tall and strong, anger flashing across her usually kind face. For a split second, Katherine saw a little bit of her mother's strength and determination in Emma's eyes.

"Momma," Emma finally whispered. "I'm so sorry for what he did to you. I can't imagine. Thank you for keeping me. Thank you for loving me in spite of the way I was conceived." Emma held Katherine in her arms until they could cry no more.

~ ~ ~

After their tears dried and promises were made to leave this discussion for another day, Katherine walked along the same stretch of road she'd walked just before she was abducted. The ditch where Casey hit his head was nearly covered by overgrown brush. Cold mountain water rushed fast toward the MacCallister's front alfalfa fields, flooding the tiny, tender stalks with life.

The things she'd learned from Martha at Cook's medicine counter brought guilt and shame over her, even though she'd had no control over what happened to her. She was thankful no one in town recognized her. Too many questions rolled around in her own mind to answer, much less dealing with theirs.

She was soothed by the familiar scents of sage and jasmine, hay and horses. Even in her sadness and the haze of her throbbing head, the sights and smells and sounds of home made her feel whole and alive for the first time in twenty years. They were memories, *not* hallucinations.

The sadness of losing Momma that way didn't make sense in her mind. Even with the nuances of thought still fuzzy from the drugs, she remembered Momma as a strong and smart matriarch. There had to be something more that drove her insane. Didn't there?

And then she remembered Augie. How Momma had reacted when Augie pulled away. The whispers of madness that floated in the room the day she found Momma crying and desperate, worried what life would bring without Augie to protect her.

"Emma," she said.

Her daughter held her hand as they walked in silence. "Yes, Momma?"

"I need to go to John first. I need to see him before I walk through this door."

Emma brought Katherine's hand to her lips and kissed it lightly on the back. "Well, let's go then. You rest. I'll drive."

"I don't even know which facility he's in." Katherine realized.

Emma guided her mother back to the passenger side and pulled open the door. "We'll search every single one 'til we find him. That's easy enough."

She closed the door, trotted around the front of the car and jumped in. Another adventure to the past. Thank God for Emma.

~ ~ ~

With each mile, a new memory surfaced. With each memory, Katherine's hate for Casey grew. He'd stolen her life. Her children had grown up without her. And she'd lost John, maybe forever.

Casey would come for them. For her. She knew it as sure as she knew that no matter what she said or what she did, those precious twenty years were lost to her forever.

Would John forgive her? Would he believe her? Would he even recognize her at all?

After touring five care facilities in Colorado Springs, Katherine started to lose hope she'd ever find him at all. She didn't dare call Ruby Marie and ask. That wasn't an option. She had to find him and see for herself. And then she'd go to her children and pray they'd accept her back.

Emma was a genius at getting past the gate keeper. She told each administrator she was a nurse looking to relocate to Colorado Springs. It so happened El Paso County was in short supply of good nurses so they happily gave tours, never once suspecting their true goal was finding a particular resident.

By the sixth stop, Katherine's head pounded. The over bright fluorescent lighting knifed straight into her temples. She needed fresh air, a comfortable place to sit and a few moments to close her eyes.

"Emma, honey, I'm gonna be out by this delightful pond while you look around. Do you mind?" She didn't wait for her a response, certain Emma would recognize John strictly from her depictions in the paintings. She pushed out the door to the small garden and took in a breath of the cool, sweet air.

The sound of water falling gently into the pond mixed with the soothing strum of a guitar calmed her the moment she sat on the comfortable chaise lounge. Ducks swam and flapped their feathers, squawking at one another in warning.

Katherine laid against the back of the chair and rested a moment, thankful to be out of the car and away from the chaos. Her hope of finding John waned.

The gentle breeze floating across the water brought with it a familiar, comforting scent. Musk and leather, and man. Her man. She knew without looking he watched her.

The singsong of his voice sounded exactly the same as when she last heard him speak her name. "Katherine?" The voice caught before saying it again. "Oh, dear God, Katherine. Is that you or have I died and gone to heaven?" The singsong was full of tears.

"John?"

He stood every bit as rugged and handsome as the last time she saw him. Gray-tipped hair, and barely a crease showed around the sparkle in his bright blue eyes.

She struggled to see him through the tears. He dropped to his knees in front of her and laid his head in her lap. And then he cried. And cried. His chest heaved against her as he wrapped his arms around and pulled her tight into him.

Katherine laced her fingers into his hair and kissed the top of his head. A hundred kisses.

She brought his face up to look into his eyes. Her soul lived there in that brilliant blue. It was that missing piece. That first night she saw him at the Sawgrass dance flashed through her mind. How mesmerizing he was to her then. How mesmerizing he remained.

"Oh, John, I'm so sorry." She kissed his lips tenderly. "I-I don't know where to start."

He sat down next to her and lifted her easily into his lap, as strong as always. When she started to speak again, he touched his finger to her lips. "Please Katherine—" His voice caught again. "I don't wanna hear where you've been or why you left. I want this dream to never end."

Chapter 45

No one was home when they got back to Ruby's Ranch. A set of gorgeous Labradors guarded the door as curious horses grazed in the front corral across the path from a new greenhouse. Momma must've been rooting vegetables and trees in there, she thought to herself. And then she turned toward the house. The house she'd always hoped to escape as a child now filled her heart with sense of home.

John leaned in to kiss her cheek. "I'll be out here, honey. You call if you need me." When he laced his long legs through the fence, the horses surrounded him and swished their flirtatious tails. The dogs rushed in to add their greeting. John chuckled when they nuzzled in for a scratch. If anything could bring him back to reality, it was being home with these glorious, forgiving creatures.

The key was in the usual hiding place behind the rusted pot on the porch. Katherine was struck silent when she walked through the door. Ruby Marie had created a regular *Home and Garden* miracle with Momma's old ranch house. No more hideous pink walls, or outdated wallpaper. The wooden floors and cabinets shined from fresh stain. The chrome on the old stove gleamed like new. Momma's kitchen clock still ticked loud and strong.

Katherine picked up the picture of her father from the mantel and held it to her chest. She missed him so very much. She couldn't believe he hadn't crossed her mind for almost twenty years. His loss hit her like it'd happened only yesterday.

"Can I see Momma?" Emma asked. "Is this your daddy? Is this the man from the stories?"

"Yes, sweetheart. This is your Grandpa Mac. I wish so much you could've met him. He was an amazing man." She handed Emma the frame and walked down the hall. The pathetic painting of her yellow orchids still hung above the table, as it had all those years ago. She wondered what kind of man her sweet Jake had become when she touched the bowed wall behind the painting.

"Oh, Momma, I'm so sorry," she whispered as Augie came to comfort her from every direction.

The door to the room she'd shared with John bounced gently against the jamb. "I've missed you too, my friend."

"Beware, child," came a voice inside her mind. It wasn't the greeting she'd expected. It was a warning from long ago.

"Oh, God." She backed away from the door, more frustrated than scared. "I'm not afraid, Augie. There's nothing anyone can do to hurt me anymore."

"Beware," the voice came again and then Augie was gone.

Katherine ran up the hall and yelled for John and Emma. "We need to find Stan and right now." She left out that she feared Casey was on the property waiting for his chance for revenge.

~ ~ ~

She found Stan in the barn, bent over a raised hoof, singing a sad John Denver song at the top of his lungs. A bright-eyed appie colt leaned against his back, begging to play.

Katherine watched quietly at first. Stan shooed the ornery colt away, then went back to filing the mare's hoof. The colt's little pink muzzle let out a loud snort then he leaned against him again, nipping at his pant leg.

"Fate, I said, get, you little fart," he said, bumping the colt on the hind quarters with his hip.

Katherine couldn't stifle her giggle.

Thankfully, Stan had a strong heart. After a double-take, he seemed to trust what his eyes told him. She could see reality register on his sad, tired face and read his thoughts. Katherine was alive and home, or he'd lost his damn mind.

"Stan," she said quietly to avoid spooking him and the horses. The colt turned on his heels and bobbed his head in Katherine's directly. Annoyed at being surprised, no doubt.

Katherine took two steps closer and scratched the colt behind the ears, then down his nose. "You're something else, aren't you, little man?" She talked to the colt but watched Stan as he worked it over in his mind.

"Katherine? Honey? Is it really you?" He sounded a hundred years old. His bloodshot eyes looked to have cried a river. He missed Momma, Katherine knew. And now he must be wondering if he loved Katherine or hated her for causing the woman he loved such pain.

She patted the feisty colt on the rump to move him away. Stan dropped the horse's hoof to the ground and leaned against the strong mare. He rubbed his eyes to focus. This time she was but a step away.

He reached for her to be sure she was solid. He jerked when he found her human and shaking.

"I'm real, Stan. I'm alive."

Stan pushed off from the mare and took Katherine in his arms. He held her there for a good five minutes before another word was spoken, sobbing against the side of her head. He touched her hair and then backed away and took her hands and looked at them.

"You are here. You're really here. Thank the lord. Oh, honey—I'm so glad you're safe. I wish your poor Momma would've been here to see you come home." He sniffled against the sadness that held him captive.

"Stan, I need your help. There's so much to tell you. So much to explain, but right now I need you more than ever before."

"What is it, honey? What can I do?" He perked up when he recognized her anxiety.

"Casey'll be coming for me, Stan. He'll be looking to hurt someone if he has to."

Stan stepped back, perplexed. "Casey? You mean Casey who worked here at the ranch?"

She nodded and pursed her lips to avoid crying. "He kidnapped me, Stan. He drugged me and brainwashed me and took me away from my life, my family."

"Oh, dear God." Guilt passed over his face. He'd trusted Casey—and felt sorry for him when he got hurt in the accident. "We checked in with his momma when you went missing. She'd said he was long gone, working some ranch up in Montana. We never thought twice about him. I feel so ignorant. I shoulda followed up on that better."

Her heart swelled knowing they'd searched so hard to find her.

"You wouldn't have found us, Stan. I guarantee his momma never knew where he really was. We moved all over, but we lived in New York much of the time—SoHo to be exact. It doesn't matter now. I think he's here. Somewhere. Probably watching us now."

"Here? Would he be that bold? He should know we'll protect you with everything we have."

"He's a sick man. He changed after the accident, something snapped in his mind."

Stan took her by the hand again and led her out into the corral. "Let's go find the little bastard then. Ain't no sense in waiting for him to come around to us. He's not getting you again, Kat. I promise you that."

"Stan, wait." She tugged at his arm to stop him. "John's

with me. I brought him home where he belongs. And my Emma."

He evaluated her words before responding, something he learned to do a long time ago dealing with Momma. "Emma?"

She smiled with pride. "She's my baby girl."

"Baby girl? Not sure how Ruby's gonna take to that. She Casey's child, Kat?"

"No, sir." She left it at that and prayed he would too.

Chapter 46

Katherine knew where Casey would be. He'd be at the circle, recharging for the task at hand. She left John in Emma's capable hands and led Stan on horseback up the ridge path, this time with Daddy's faithful six-shooter strapped to her saddlebag.

"Child, are you sure we should be leaving them back there with John's condition and all? What if Casey's trying to draw us out so he can get to them? To hurt you?"

She chuckled quietly. "There ain't nothing wrong with John that some good loving won't fix. I'm sure he'll handle Casey just fine if he's stupid enough to show up there."

"Oh hell, Kat. I don't need to hear all that. That boy went plumb crazy when you disappeared. I'm not sure which of 'em were worse off, your Momma or him."

At the top of Haley's Peak, Katherine took in the expanse of Ruby's Ranch. Everything had grown and matured. More buildings and more cattle. Horses and colts filled the corrals.

"Looks like the place has done real well, Stan."

"It kept your Momma alive as long as she was, Kat. Plus, your girl has really cleaned things up since she took over. The men respect her. She's got grit."

"Just like Momma." She stated, rather than asked.

"Yessum, just like your momma." He smiled a distant smile. "She's had herself a little help."

"Help? Ruby Marie?" She caught his eye, curious.

"You remember that little MacCallister boy, Billy?" He reined his horse in next to hers and looked over the valley.

A smile stretched across her face remembering the full head of hair with an adorable little boy under it.

"Well, he definitely ain't no little boy no more. He and your girl, they got something special going on between 'em. It's a beautiful thing. He's helped her come to terms with a lot—coming home to all this mess. He loves her, Kat. There ain't no hiding it. Seems to me he's always loved her. She's been struggling to understand what happened to you and what happened to your momma. She won't let it rest. She's a smart one. Stubborn as the day is long but I think he's gotten to 'er. God knows I hope so. He's a good man." He patted the chestnut quarter on the withers and urged him to head up the trail.

Katherine smiled again, this time recalling the adoring look that little boy always had for her Ruby Marie. "Well, ain't that something," she said. "Love does persevere, after all. I had a feeling he'd win her over one day."

When they reached the clover and the thicket of trees, to her great surprise, Stan led the way to the circle. She slid off the horse and patted her, missing her beautiful Cricket.

"So, you knew about this place? All that time?" She followed him.

"I knew soon enough. I knew your Momma disappeared up here a lot. Then once she wasn't able to bring herself, she asked me to bring 'er. She had to make peace, I suppose."

Katherine stood next to him outside the circle. "And did she?" She asked. "Did she make peace?"

"Only God in heaven knows, Kat. It was the damnedest thing I'd ever witnessed. It did seem to calm her down, so I suppose that's a gift." He didn't look at her when he talked.

Across the circle, something moved quickly behind the brush. A glint of light shined in her eyes.

"That'll be Casey," she said. "I'll have to take it from here."

She entered the circle, watchful for Casey to show himself. When she touched the center rock, the light enveloped her in energy. It was the safest place on the ranch for her and she knew it, but Casey had the power to break through the light. She remembered him sitting cross-legged on this very spot the night he kidnapped her. But how could he be part of the light, when his heart was so dark?

"Kat," he called out, pain evident in his voice. "Kat please, come home with me? You don't belong here—you never did. I gave you what you wanted. Wasn't ours a good life? You're an artist and you live in the city like you always dreamed. Please, come home with me. We can forget this happened."

He crossed the outside barrier and inched closer to her. Glimmers from the light sparked toward him like tiny lightning strikes. He held out his hands beckoning the light to take him, but it held only Katherine in its grasp.

And then the shaman appeared. When Casey tried to reach through the beam to pull her free, the energy burned his hand.

"Please, Kat. Let me in. Please?" He fell to his knees outside the circle of light. He was a desperate man. He loved her, she knew. But what a terrible, sick kind of love.

She felt sorry for him as his heart broke in his chest. The more sympathy she had for him, the dimmer the light became, and the more transparent the shaman appeared.

"Casey, please, leave me be. I love John. I always have. What you did to me was a horrible, abusive thing. You need help." Tears rolled down her cheeks as the light and protective barrier disappeared.

Casey stood and held his hand out to her—begging for her to come with him, willingly. When she shook her head, and backed away, he lunged and grabbed her by the hair. "You're coming with me one way or the other, Kat." Hurt became anger.

"I don't think so!" John's singsong voice was serious and fearsome. For the first time, he walked boldly into the circle. "Let my wife go, Casey. Now!"

"She was never your wife. You never deserved her." Casey pulled Katherine to him and held her tight.

John watched him intently. His eyes trained directly on Casey's. "You don't want to do this."

Katherine yelled, "Casey, let me go. I don't want you. I never wanted you." She struggled to get away.

Her twist to the side gave John a shot. In a flash, Casey was on the ground with a bullet hole through his head, and Katherine clung as tightly as she could to John, sobbing into his chest. Thankful it was over. Thankful she was home.

As John escorted Katherine out of the circle, the light and the shaman reappeared over Casey's body. Katherine, John, and Stan watched in amazement as the luminous figure picked up Casey's limp body and disappeared. No trace of blood or deception remained.

They stood speechless, looking from one to the other. Then Stan finally said, "Someone's definitely gonna explain this to me one day. Definitely."

Chapter 47

"I'm gonna take a ride out to the cemetery. I need to visit my parents' graves to say a proper goodbye." Katherine sat up on the side of the bed and patted John's leg. "You rest, sweetheart. I'll be back soon."

"Katherine," he asked, drowsily. "You sure you don't want me to go?"

She looked back and smiled. "I'll be okay. Emma will drive me. I'm not going anywhere. I promise you I'm never gonna leave you again."

Those words seemed to soothe him.

Augie floated in the air outside the bedroom when she closed the door behind her.

"Thank you, Augie. Watch over him for me." She spoke quietly.

His embrace was as real as if he were human. Much like the embrace which took Casey away. Someday, she knew the mystery of Augie and the circle would reveal itself, but for now she felt secure and whole again. She had nothing more to beware. She was finally safe, and home.

Katherine jumped into the passenger seat of the rental car and smiled at Emma, ever steady by her side. She would find a way to tell her what happened to Casey, but not now. Not yet.

"Ready, Momma?" she asked through a smile.

"Ready," she smiled back, marveling at how the willows lining the driveway had grown.

"This drive is so beautiful. Those trees are amazing."

Emma stuck her head out the open window to gaze at the lush, green canopy above their heads.

Every billow of the leaves made Katherine think of her father. How she loved him. How she missed him. The breeze lifting the fragile limbs made her feel like he watched her from above, so happy she finally made her way back home. "Daddy planted them when I was born."

"Ahhhh, that's beautiful. Sounds like Grandpa Mac was a romantic." Emma stated, clutching her mother's hand.

"That's an understatement."

~ ~ ~

Momma was buried next to Daddy on the far hill of Green Valley Cemetery. The fresh dirt covering Momma's grave was starkly different than the flower covered headstone that read simply, *Mac Adams. Beloved husband, father, rancher. One of life's' true gentlemen.* She still couldn't believe she didn't make it home in time to ease Momma's mind. This would be a regret until the day she died.

"I'm sorry, Momma," she whispered. "At least you and Daddy are finally together." She placed the handful of roses she'd plucked from Momma's garden on each headstone. "I hope you're finally happy." She sat on the cool grass that grew between them and placed one hand on each grave, connecting with her parents after all the lost years.

Emma let her be for a long while, even after Katherine laid down to soak in the warmth of the sun. This was as peaceful a visit as she'd ever had with her parents and for once, Momma had to listen to what she had to say.

Quiet footsteps of two, maybe three people came toward her from where Emma sat in the car. As much as Katherine wanted to keep her eyes closed and her mind free, she had to see who was coming.

A tall, handsome cowboy and a short blonde woman walked toward her together with Emma. The resemblance between the three couldn't be denied. Katherine knew before they got within twenty feet this was Billy and Claudie MacCallister. There could be no doubt.

She stood to face them, unsure what kind of reception she'd receive from Nancy MacCallister's children. She realized every person she faced after all these years could bring a different result. There would be disbelievers. How could she have lived for so long in darkness? Why did she not remember?

"Katherine?" Billy spoke first. He looked her over to be certain in his own mind this was truly his Ruby's long-lost mother.

She smiled at him, amazed. She could see his love for her daughter shine through his cautious perusal. "Yes, Billy. I'm Katherine." She stepped forward to give him a better look.

Claudie spoke next. "Ruby and Jake have gone to find out what's happened to their dad. Is he with you?" She stepped in front of her brother and met Katherine's eyes. Searching, protective.

"He's at the ranch. He's home."

"Ruby was devastated when you disappeared. Now you've come back out of thin air. If you're here to hurt her, I'll kindly ask you to leave before she gets home. Neither she nor Jake deserves that kind of cruelty." Billy's eyes were damp with concern but his threat was sincere.

Katherine glanced at her mother's head stone again and nodded. "I'm glad she's had all of you to take care of her. I assure you I'm not here to hurt my children. It'll take time to explain what kept me from my family. Time and understanding."

"I hope you're not expecting her to rush into your arms," Claudie added.

"Momma's not expecting anything of the sort. You don't

know what she's been through. None of you realize what horrible things she's been through." Emma flared up.

Billy looked Emma square in the eye, then back to Katherine. "Did she call you, Momma?"

"Billy, Claudie—this is Emma. My daughter. And your sister."

All three of the younger people took a step back and gawked at Katherine with shock.

"I may as well start my story now. Your father . . ." She halted, considering how best to share this information. "He . . ." She chose her words carefully. "He may have thought he was . . . comforting me. I didn't . . . consent, but we made a baby. A beautiful baby. And this is my Emma."

Claudie huffed and crossed her arms. "Daddy's always willing to 'comfort,' isn't he?"

"Claudie, stop." Billy scolded her.

"It's true. He's a man whore. And now this. This will kill our mom. And Ruby—how is she gonna feel about this?"

Emma stood quietly, looking more to support her mother than to make this news okay for her new siblings.

Billy raked his hands through his chestnut hair and let out a deep breath.

"Do any of you mind keeping this little nugget of information quiet until after Ruby and Jake come out of shock from Katherine coming back from the dead?" He looked from one to the other to the other and forced their answer.

"I agree, Billy. I don't want my Ruby hurt anymore," Katherine consented.

"Let's get you to the ranch," he said. "They're on their way back now."

Chapter 48

Katherine busied herself making gingerbread cookies to keep from rattling out of her shoes. Nerves trembled as her children neared the ranch. Emma tried to calm her, but guilt crept over her like a dark cloud. How would she ever make Ruby and Jake understand when she was still trying to come to grips?

She set the cookies to cool on the wire racks and wiped her damp hands on the apron. Out the window, she spied the greenhouse once again, and she was curious.

When she walked to the porch, she noticed steam on the high windows of the beautifully crafted glass house.

"What the devil?" She crossed the dirt driveway and opened the heavy metal door that enclosed the damp space. When the steam cleared she was shocked to see a thousand beautiful orchids setting atop stacked shelves lining the entire building. A thousand frivolous flowers—as Momma would say.

Tears and steam mixed with the first of her wailing cries. She could feel how broken Momma must've been to keep her daughter close, if only in her beloved orchids.

She sat in the rocking chair at the center of the ocean of colored blooms, and cried and cried. Momma was gone but she'd left the kindest part of her heart here in this greenhouse. A tribute of sorts. Of all the things Momma had ever done to help her and protect her, this was by far the most impactful to Katherine's wounded heart.

She worked in the greenhouse for hours, plucking dead blossoms from the wiry green stalks. Each pot was given a sprinkle of food, and a splash of water, before she sat again to marvel at the majesty.

She didn't notice when everyone left the ranch or when the car carrying her children came and went without her knowing.

Katherine worked to gather herself before the inevitable confrontation that was to come.

~ ~ ~

The creak of the heavy metal door woke Katherine from a fitful sleep. A younger version of John searched through the steam to find her. It was her Jake, she knew it. She would recognize him anywhere.

"I'm here," she called.

"Momma?" His voice was deep and strong.

She stood from her chair when he approached. No words came to her mind to say. She only watched his face as he searched over her every feature, as if to be sure she was really his mother.

"Jake, sweetheart. Is that you?" She placed her hand on his cheek.

His eyes were alight with excitement and acceptance. His heart open. When he bent down to hug her, she felt a quiver in his chest. "I'm so glad you've come home," he said.

"So am I, sweetheart. So am I."

"You're gonna have to give Ruby some time, Momma. She's angry, and hurt about all of this."

Katherine settled back in the rocking chair and contemplated. "We'll work through this together, Jake. All of us. We have the rest of our lives to figure it all out."

Jake flipped over an empty five-gallon bucket and sat to talk. He didn't want to know why she'd left or how it happened. He wanted to know where she'd been and why she'd come home.

Katherine was proud and amazed at what a secure, calm human being he'd turned out to be after being such a skittish child.

"It was Ruby," he said. "She took care of me. She raised me while Daddy worked. When his depression would take over, she got him moving again. Daddy and I both owe our lives to Ruby."

Katherine listened as he regaled her with the years of living and maturing. Told her of his wife and her beautiful twin grandbabies. She ached for the years she'd missed watching him grow up.

Chapter 49

An hour later, the metal door creaked open so quietly, Katherine wasn't sure she'd heard it at all. Steam gathered around a statuesque young woman with strawberry blonde hair. Emma followed close behind.

Katherine slowly stood from her chair, anticipating. Afraid.

"Let me talk to her, Momma," Jake said quietly. And he walked to greet his sister at the door.

She couldn't quite make out the mumbled conversation, but she could sense the tension. It took all her strength and determination to walk the twenty or so feet toward her daughter. To prove to her she was alive and ready to resume her role.

Emma rushed to her mother's side. Katherine was thankful for her support.

The woman who stood in front of her only slightly resembled the teenage girl she'd left behind. Her flowing strawberry blonde hair pulled tight into a ponytail at the back of her head accentuated the high cheekbones and curious almond eyes. Her sun-kissed skin was no longer covered with freckles.

They watched each other for a long moment before either said a word.

"Momma?" Ruby Marie reached for Katherine to be sure she wasn't a vision. Afraid to believe, to hope, that her mother had come back to them after all these years.

Pain and anger festered in Ruby's eyes. These were the eyes of someone who felt abandoned. She'd been left to deal with everyone's sorrow, while her flighty mother gallivanted around the world, living her own dreams.

But that was only partly true. She'd lived out the dream of painting and living a city life, but it would never be worth losing her family.

When Ruby started to turn and run, Jake caught her arm. "Ruby," he said. "Try to hear her out."

She just glanced between him and the vision that was her mother.

Jake repeated. "Try. You can do this Ruby. You're the strongest person I know. Show her how brave you are. Remember something, remember you've always been the brave one. Daddy and I could never have made it without you. For that I'll be eternally grateful."

"And so will I," Katherine agreed, sliding her hand into Ruby's, hoping for forgiveness or at least a chance to explain.

It was too much, too soon for her daughter. Ruby Marie pulled her hand away and was gone out the door and into the house as Jake and Emma called after her.

Katherine's heart sank. She'd lost her daughter in this tragedy. If she was going to ever make amends, she'd have to be patient and understanding of what Ruby had been through.

"Well, I can't leave it like this," she said to Jake and Emma. "We all have to eat." She grabbed the basket from the wooden potting bench and picked fresh fruits and vegetables for dinner. When she entered the kitchen, she was careful to give her daughter space.

"I hope you don't mind, I picked these for supper," she said as she placed the vine-ripened tomatoes into the colander to wash. "They're ready to eat."

"That's fine," her daughter answered quietly as she tore lettuce and through it in the blue willow bowl. "I planned to pick a few for the salad, anyway."

They worked in silence together as if they hadn't missed an evening in the last twenty years. Each followed techniques passed down to them from Momma.

Katherine caught Ruby staring when she cut the tomatoes, but she didn't say a word. Her daughter was like a frightened rabbit, unsure if she was a wolf or a carrot.

Katherine gave her another moment before adding. "I made some gingerbread cookies this morning. I hope you don't mind. I thought we might have them for dessert." She paused. ". . . if that's okay with you?"

Ruby Marie kept working with her lasagna, keeping her eyes trained away from her mother. "Sure, that's fine."

Katherine took her agreement as a huge success though she knew Ruby's emotions bubbled very near the surface. More questions would come, some hateful, some mournful, but she'd remain patient, praying her daughter would one day open her heart and truly understand.

They would go to bed this night without a mention of Katherine's journey through hell and how she'd made it back home. Ruby Marie seemed to take more from seeing her father happy again. He laughed and reminisced with Stan and the others at the table, like they'd never missed a day. Daddy and Jake even exchanged a long embrace, making up for lost time.

Katherine knew there was something to John's diagnosis, otherwise why would he be so accepting of her now? But she didn't care. They were all together again around Momma's big oak table. Dysfunction had always been part of the mystique of Ruby's Ranch. It wouldn't be home without it.

"Whattya say we get married, Katherine?" John whispered as he wrapped his long arm around her waist and kissed her cheek. "I think it's high time I make an honest woman of you, don't you?"

Katherine placed her hand over his on the table then bent

in to gently kiss the lips that she'd missed for so long. She fell into the safety of the deep blue of his eyes and smiled.

Tears streamed down Ruby Marie's beautiful face as she witnessed the true love her parents' shared. When she reached across the table and placed her hand atop theirs, Katherine knew everything was finally going to be all right. "I'd love that more than anything in the world. Mrs. John Lattrell does have a ring to it."

If you enjoyed this story, please go online to Amazon.com and post a review.

Also by **Rhonda Frankhauser**
and **Soul Mate Publishing**:

RETURN TO RUBY'S RANCH

Ruby Lattrell inherited Ruby's Ranch after the death of her grandmother. Before she can begin to live her own life, she has to answer the questions that have haunted her for the two decades since her father dragged her away from the only true home she had ever known. What really happened to her beloved mother? And what drove her poor Granny Rube insane?

When Ruby returns to the ranch, her chance at true happiness comes in the form of a handsome cowboy named Billy McCallister—who has loved her since they were kids. Will the truth about her mother come between them? In the end, Ruby finds all of her answers with the shocking death of someone dear, and a surreal family reunion that will give the reader unrelenting hope for happy endings.

Available now on Amazon: <u>RETURN TO RUBY'S RANCH</u>

HEALTH NUT CAFÉ

Imagine recognizing someone you've never seen before…

Becka Clemmons' one true passion is running the Health Nut Café. Awakened every morning by the same nightmare, Becka sees the world through tainted eyes. She's never believed in fairytale romances until Jonathan Parker walks through the café door one cool, foggy morning. She struggles to understand why this familiar stranger makes her crave things she's never craved. Solving the mystery of

Jonathan is the first thing that has ever taken her focus away from her café.

Imagine missing someone you've never met…

Jonathan Parker is the idealistic son of old money who knows exactly what he wants. Day after day, he searches to find the missing connection that eludes him, until the morning he lays eyes on Becka. He knows his search is over but the struggle to make her believe has just begun. From that moment, he works to prove to Becka that they belong together.

Will Becka let herself believe? Will Jonathan's family ruin their chance at love?

Available now on Amazon: HEALTH NUT CAFÉ